SHOOT-OUT AT OWL CREEK

With a law star in his pocket and a gun in his holster, Kell Bannon rides into the Big Bend country of Texas to set up the Parfitt gang for capture. Prepared for a shoot-out, he faces more trouble with Clarkville's crooked Sheriff Bixby; the aggressive ranch foreman, Piercey; and Mack Jex, boss of the local rustling business. It's tough work, and for Bannon, he knows that only his deadly gun and quick shooting can bring a satisfactory result.

CORBA SUNMAN

SHOOT-OUT AT OWL CREEK

Complete and Unabridged

LINFORD
Leicester

First published in Great Britain in 2007 by
Robert Hale Limited
London

First Linford Edition
published 2008
by arrangement with
Robert Hale Limited
London

British Library CIP Data

Sunman, Corba
    Shoot-out at Owl Creek.—Large print ed.—
Linford western library
    1. Western stories
    2. Large type books
    I. Title
    823.9'2 [F]

    ISBN 978–1–84782–435–6

Published by
F. A. Thorpe (Publishing)
Anstey, Leicestershire

Set by Words & Graphics Ltd.
Anstey, Leicestershire
Printed and bound in Great Britain by
T. J. International Ltd., Padstow, Cornwall

This book is printed on acid-free paper

1

It was always a big event in the calendar of Governor of the State of Texas Franklyn C. Mayhew, when the notorious outlaw-cum-lawman, Kell Bannon, showed up in his office to talk about the outlaw question. Mayhew controlled a select band of special state deputy marshals with the thankless and very dangerous job of policing the vast area west of the Pecos River and down along the Rio Grande, where the lawless element seemed to outnumber the honest pioneers pushing steadily into the fertile south-west. Bannon, whose face was well known along the border for his infamous exploits, had the price of 2000 dollars, dead or alive, on his head, but was, in fact, Mayhew's most able undercover marshal whose alleged criminal activities under his cloak of pseudo-lawlessness had contributed greatly to the success of the governor's special interest.

Darkness had fallen when Bannon was shown into Mayhew's office to confront his superior. Mayhew arose from his desk and advanced around it with outstretched hand, his fleshy face registering great pleasure. Of medium build, Mayhew, at fifty-two, had become the scourge of the outlaws who plied their callous business along the back trails where civilization was still tenuous and honest folk went in fear of their lives.

'Bannon, it's always a pleasure to see you.' Mayhew shook hands warmly.

'Likewise, Governor.' Kell Bannon had enormous respect for the man who fought an unceasing battle against the wrongdoers in the Lone Star state. 'I'm sure glad that last chore came out the way you said it would. I said my prayers more than once before I finally got Abe Doolin and his bunch dead to rights. It was a real tough chore, and no mistake, but I didn't get a scratch in that little ruckus and I expect you've got something else lined up for me to tackle now.'

Bannon was big, raw-boned, powerful, and looked like a man who could handle himself in any situation. He was twenty-five, dressed in dusty range clothes — a blue shirt, faded blue denim pants protected by Texas leg chaps, and a dark leather vest. Black hair showed from under the brim of his black Stetson and his cold brown eyes were unblinking, filled with a brightness that testified to his abhorrence of the bad men with whom he was linked. A yellow neckerchief was tied around his throat, and the black cartridge-belt around his waist had a greased holster containing a well-used Colt .45.

'Bannon, you've always managed to pull off the chores that even the Texas Rangers have failed at, but at last we come to the big one.' Mayhew's face took on a grim expression as he turned and pointed at the large-scale map of Texas on the wall behind his desk.

Bannon moved in beside his superior, his keen eyes following the line of the Rio Grande, which marked their western boundary. Mayhew reached out and tapped the map where the Rio Grande turned north to form what was known as the Big Bend. 'The border gangs along the river are stronger than ever. Not only are they rustling both sides of the border, they are hitting banks in Texas and getting away with thousands of dollars.'

'I've heard about the situation in that area,' Bannon observed, his eyes narrowing as he recalled all he knew about south-western lawlessness. 'I reckon it would take an army to make any progress against the gangs.'

'And all I have are one alleged outlaw, and ten special marshals who will ride to hell and gone to back him up once he's done the dirty work of setting up the bandits,' Mayhew said drily. 'If you feel equal to this chore, Bannon, head for the town of Clarkville. Here it is.' He tapped the map with a long forefinger. 'That seems to be the headquarters of the gang handling most of the bank-robbing. Ride in as Kell Bannon on the dodge and find out what you can about the gang. There's talk that Hemp Parfitt is running the bunch causing all the trouble in that area. Find out what you can, set up the gang, and warn me in time to get marshals into position to catch them red-handed. We can only hit these gangs individually, but I don't have to tell you what's to be done, and there's no time limit on the job. Parfitt's gang is the toughest on the border so he's the one to start with.'

'How do I get word to you when the time is right to strike?' Bannon asked.

'That's a good question.' Mayhew grimaced. 'Communication is always a big problem, huh? There's a little cattle ranch working under the JG brand just outside Clarkville, where Jake Garner lives. Garner is an ex-marshal and is my eyes and ears in that area. He took in a girl named Bella Thompson after his wife died, and she's also working for me. She's the widow of another of our men, Bill Thompson, who was killed in Clarkville last year — he was working undercover against Parfitt and fell foul of Mack Jex, a property developer who seems to be implicated in the rustling that's rife in the area. Bella went as a saloon-girl, got mixed up against her will with Jex, and went to live with Garner ostensibly to mother Garner's son, Cal, aged ten. She'll take messages from you and pass them on to me. You'll have to introduce yourself to her by mentioning my name. That's all I can do for you, Bannon. The rest is up to you. Just remember that killing Parfitt won't end the threat of his gang. We have to get every last one of those bad men dead to rights, so get among them, learn their habits, and set them up for the rest of the men to come in riding and shooting.'

'I'll get moving then.' Bannon was aware of what had to be done and knew the odds against his success were too great to contemplate. He studied the map for a moment longer before turning away with narrowed eyes. 'Be seeing you, Governor. I'll hit the Mexican border in about two weeks.'

'There's one thing more.' Mayhew turned to his desk and picked up a thin sheaf of posters. 'These are the latest descriptions of some of the men who form the nucleus of Parfitt's gang. All are known killers, and they don't hesitate to murder their way through the robberies they commit. They are bad men, Bannon, and have to be put down like the animals they are.'

Bannon took the posters and riffled through them for his first glimpse of Hemp Parfitt and his crooked sidekicks. Tough faces peered up at him from dim photographs. 'They're a real bad bunch and no mistake!' he observed drily. 'OK, I'll get on their trail.'

They shook hands and Bannon departed, losing himself in the shadows and departing as silently as he had arrived. He rode into the great south-west, moving steadily and mile after dusty mile slipped by under the tireless hoofs of his big black horse. His right hand never strayed far from the pistol on his hip, for it contained the only law that would exist when he reached his destination.

Bannon rode through a wilderness of mesquite and cactus desert, finding little grass and few settlements. A single railroad track traversed the empty plains, and villages and sparse towns had grown up along the right of way where weary pioneers had decided to put down roots and settle, their communities subsisting on the flourishing cattle industry.

Two weeks of steady riding brought Bannon within sight of Jake Garner's little cow spread near Clarkville. He reined in when he saw the JG sign over the gateway to the dusty yard, and spent a long time looking at the large cabin, the corral behind it, and the four-square barn off to the left, close to a creek. The shadows of approaching night deepened imperceptibly and darkness began to stray into hollows and corners before he moved in closer to rein up beside the dead man sprawled in front of the half-open door of the cabin. Silence pressed in heavily and the surrounding range seemed devoid of life.

The dead man, aged about fifty, lay on his face in the careless attitude of sudden death, his left knee slightly bent, both arms out-flung, his head turned to one side with wide eyes staring sightlessly into the setting sun. He was dressed in ranch work clothes and was not wearing a hat. A large bloodstain showed on the back of his shirt where he had been shot — right between the shoulder-blades.

Bannon stepped down from his saddle and trailed his reins. His right hand was close to the butt of his holstered pistol as he bent over the man and gazed into the set features, taking in facial details. Then he sighed deeply and straightened.

'Jake Garner, I guess,' he said softly, his lips twisting with unaccustomed emotion.

The sound of hoofs rattling on hard ground some way off jerked him into movement. He swung to face the direction from which the disturbance sounded, but the shadows were too thick now to permit sight of the newcomer. The echoing thud of hoofs drew closer, and Bannon counted at least three horses approaching. He moved to his black, took up the reins, and led the animal around the left side of the cabin to leave it out of sight before going back to the front corner of the building and remaining there.

Three riders appeared out of the gloom and came openly to the cabin.

'Where in hell are you, Jake?' one of them called as they reined up.

'It ain't like him to sit in the dark,' another remarked.

'Someone is down on the stoop,' the third observed.

The trio dismounted and crowded forward. One of them struck a match and held it close to Jake Garner's dead face. A concerted gasp arose from the newcomers.

'Heck, it is Jake,' someone observed. 'They've killed him!'

'Hold it right there,' Bannon warned, drawing his pistol and cocking it. 'I got you covered. Declare yourselves.'

'I'm Sheriff Ed Bixby out of Clarkville,' one of the trio replied immediately. 'Who in hell are you, standing out here in the dark with Jake dead on his own doorstep?'

'I got here just ahead of you and found him like that.' Bannon said flatly.

'Where are Bella and Cal? They should be somewhere around. I spoke to Jake a couple of weeks ago and he didn't mention anything about trouble, though I must admit he looked worried some.'

'I ain't seen anyone else.' Bannon lowered his gun, uncocked it and returned it to his holster.

'Some time ago Jake took in Bella Thompson, who had been hard used by Mack Jex in Clarkville. Bella has kept house for Jake, and was mothering Jake's boy, Cal.' Bixby's law badge glinted on his shirt-front as he straightened. 'Have you looked in the house? They might be dead inside.'

Bannon remained motionless while the sheriff entered the cabin. A moment later a match scraped and flared. Yellow light flooded the interior of the building, and Bixby's stocky figure moved back into the doorway.

'Place is empty,' he said. 'I wish to hell I'd got here before the sun went down. Do you reckon Bella and Cal lit out for Clarkville?'

'So what brought you here now?' Bannon remained in the shadows.

'The bank in Willow Bend was robbed yesterday. I took out after the thieves with Joe and Ike here, but we lost tracks to the north, and swung this way on the ride back to Clarkville to see if Jake had seen any sign of the robbers.'

'Mebbe the bank-robbers dropped in and did this,' Joe Renton remarked. 'They did some killing in Willow Bend that wasn't necessary.'

'It was the Parfitt gang,' said Ike Marsden. 'It had their stamp on it.'

Bannon experienced a thrill at the mention of Parfitt's name.

'We'll stick around until morning so we can look for tracks in daylight,' Bixby decided. 'Put Jake's body in the barn, boys. We'll bury him tomorrow, and mebbe we'll find some sign of Bella and young Cal. I don't know what's going on these days, but it looks like we're heading into a storm of lawless-ness. There's someone stirring up trouble all round, and we're not getting any help from state law. I wrote to the governor's office weeks ago and didn't even get a reply.'

Bixby turned and re-entered the cabin. Bannon waited until Garner's body had been removed and then entered the building. The sheriff was attending to the stove. He looked up at

13

Bannon, his faded blue eyes narrowed, glistening in the dim lamplight. He was old, maybe fifty, and his stocky frame was running to seed in the shape of a paunch. His leathery face was burned almost black by his past summers, and he grunted in suppressed pain whenever his weight rested on his left leg.

'So who are you, huh?' he demanded. 'And what's your business?'

'I'm riding through. My name is Kelly, Joe Kelly.' Bannon used his mother's maiden name.

He looked around the cabin, which was clean and showed a woman's hand in the curtains at the windows. The floor was swept, the wooden table scrubbed white, and everything was in its place. A small vase containing wild flowers was standing in the centre of the table. There was a back door which stood ajar. Bannon moved towards it, his right hand on the butt of his holstered Colt, and he was still several feet from the door when it was pushed open wide to reveal a young woman standing motionless in the shadows just outside. She was holding a rifle and the muzzle lifted instantly to gape at him.

'Who are you?' she demanded. She looked to be in her middle twenties; her long hair was golden yellow, her blue eyes filled with fierce determination. She was pretty, strongly feminine, with small features and well-shaped lips, but there were lines in her face that had nothing to do with age, and Bannon was aware that she grieved still for her dead husband.

'I'm Joe Kelly. I guess you're Bella. Where's Cal?'

'Here.' A youngster aged about ten appeared at Bella's side. He was holding a squirrel-gun in his right hand 'Where's Pa?'

Bella saw the sheriff and lowered the rifle, her expression changing.

'Jake put us in the storm cellar out back when he saw riders coming,' she said. 'We've been pestered recently by a bad crew of Mexicans who won't stay away. This time there were four of them.'

Bixby came forward from the background. 'Bella, who are those men you're talking about? Had you seen any of them before? Can you describe them? We've been tracking four riders who held up the bank two days ago in Willow Bend. It looked like they was heading this way.'

'Pa said they're bad men.' Cal Garner laid the .22 rifle on a corner of the table. 'Where is my pa?'

'He's dead — shot in the back,' Bixby said bluntly.

Cal cried out in shock and his youthful face paled. Bella grasped him and held him close, her narrowed gaze on Bannon's face. She had the stricken look of a fatally shot deer in her blue eyes and her mouth was wide in a silent O. Fresh grief filled her expression.

'I knew it would come to this,' she said slowly. 'I warned Jake what would happen but he was a stubborn man. He wouldn't seek help.'

'You'd better sit down, Bella,' Bixby

advised. 'Better yet, you can cook us some grub. I got two men with me. We'll stay until morning so I can take a look around in daylight. I'll want descriptions of the men you've seen around here lately.'

Bella nodded, put down her rifle, and turned to the stove. Bannon went to the front door.

'Where are you going?' Bixby demanded.

'Take care of my horse.'

'Where have you come from? What do you do for a living?' Bixby's eyes were narrowed. He could see certain signs about Bannon that gave him an impression of a man who lived by the big pistol snug in his holster, and made a mental note to check out the pile of wanted posters he kept in his office back in Clarkville.

Bannon left the cabin without answering. He fetched his black and led the animal over to the barn. There was an empty stall inside the building, and a water-trough just outside the big front door. He allowed the horse to drink before stabling it, and then forked hay and a scoop of oats into a trough in the stall. His thoughts were stagnant. He was shocked by the discovery of Jake Garner lying dead on his own stoop.

The two possemen had placed Jake's body in a corner of the barn and covered it with a tarp. Bannon stood motionless over the inert figure for a few moments before returning to the cabin.

The smell of cooking food assailed his nostrils when he entered the cabin and he paused. The atmosphere was tense. Cal Garner was sitting on a seat beside the stove, his gaze intent, his eyes seeing nothing. Bannon crossed to the boy's side.

'What's been going on around here, Cal?' he demanded. 'Tell me about the men who have been showing up. Did they talk to Jake about anything in particular?'

Cal shook his head. 'The only man I saw was the one who came to the cabin and talked. He didn't seem unfriendly, but Pa never asked him in or offered to feed him.'

'What did he look like? Can you remember anything? What about the horse he rode?'

'It was a bay, mebbe sixteen hands high. I never saw a bigger horse. The man was a Mex, short, no taller than Bella, and he had a mean face — cold blue eyes. He wore twin guns on crossed cartridge belts, and looked like he knew how to use them.'

'How many times did he show up, and when was the first time he came?' Bannon pursued.

'I saw him twice. The first time about two weeks ago, but his hoof-prints were in the yard more times than that, and Pa never answered questions about him. That man had to be staying somewhere close by to be able to come and go like he did.'

'Did you hear what he said to Jake?' Bannon continued patiently. 'Think hard, Cal. I'd like to know what's been going on around here.'

'I didn't hear a thing. I'm allus working about the place, and that feller came in kinda quiet. I never saw him more than twice, but I'll know him again. Do you think he killed my pa?'

'We'll take a look around in the morning and see what we can find in the way of tracks,' Bannon promised.

'I'm gonna try and find that man.' Cal's youthful face hardened as he looked up, his tone harsh. 'I ain't never killed a man yet, but I sure as hell wanta get whoever shot my pa.'

'What for you asking all those questions?' Bixby demanded. 'What's it to you what happened here? You talk like some kind of a law man. You said you're just riding through, so where are you heading? And where have you come from?'

'I'll be looking for a riding job when I hit Clarkville,' Bannon replied. 'A friend of mine named Mayhew reckoned I could find work around here.'

Bella's expression changed slightly at the mention of Mayhew's name. She looked up from the stove, her pale eyes glinting as she considered Bannon anew, taking in details of his powerful figure and regarding the big pistol holstered on his right hip. She returned her attention to the cooking food, but her shoulders were stiff and she held her head higher than before.

'We got a lot of problems in this neck of the woods,' Bixby said. 'It's more than I can cope with. I've informed the authorities that I need an army in here, but didn't even get a reply from those desk-riders up there in Austin. You don't look like a man who chases cows, mister. I reckon the only time you touch beef is when it's served to you on a plate. Ain't that so? There's plenty of work around here for a man who's handy with a gun, and I place you in that line of work. Well, you better listen to some good advice. Don't get mixed up in local trouble. There ain't no future in it. When the state governor gets around to doing something this place will be knee-deep in lawmen and we'll make a clean sweep clear to the Rio Grande.'

Bannon nodded, only half-listening to the old lawman. His ears had caught the sound outside of a steel-shod hoof cracking against a stone.

'We got company,' he rasped quickly, and his pistol seemed to leap into his hand.

Bixby moved fast. He blew out the lamp and darkness swooped in except for a dull red glow of the fire showing in the stove.

'Get down in case there's shooting,' Bixby ordered, opening the door a fraction to get a glimpse of the yard.

Bannon moved to a window overlooking the yard and peered out into the shrouding shadows. He caught the sound of a hoof on hard ground and narrowed his eyes in an attempt to pierce the darkness. A darting spurt of orange flame suddenly split the night and the boom of a Colt blasted through the silence. Bannon ducked as a bullet smashed the windowpane beside his head, showering him with jagged shards of glass. He reared up quickly, smashed his muzzle through an unbroken lower pane, and triggered his pistol as more gun-flashes followed the first. The next instant the cabin was deluged with fire, and bullets smashed into the wood-work, bored through, and crackled across the cabin in blind flight.

At least four guns were shooting indiscriminately into the building. Shadows moved deceptively as horses stamped and shied at the gunfire. Bannon fired at flashes, his eyes narrowed as he tried to pick out movement. He felt the tug of a bullet as it passed through a fold of his leather jacket, but his flesh was untouched. He thumbed back his Stetson and brack-eted the yard with questing lead until his hammer fell upon a used cartridge. He ducked below the windowsill to reload, and when he arose again the shooting had ceased and he could hear the sullen thud of receding hoofbeats fading with the dying gun echoes.

'Anyone hurt?' Bixby called from the doorway.

There was no reply inside the cabin. Bixby jerked open the cabin door and moved outside, his figure almost invisible. Bannon relaxed, content to let the local lawman handle the situation. He holstered his gun and waited patiently in the darkness for order to be restored, aware that the initiative was out of his hands — a situation he intended changing at the first opportunity.

2

The two possemen followed Bixby outside and Bella closed the door behind them before relighting the lamp. She went back to the stove and continued with her cooking. Bannon re-checked his pistol. He listened intently for sounds outside, and presently heard hoofs in the yard. Then Bixby's voice called.

'Bella, we're gonna make a sweep around to look for those fellers, and we'll head back to Clarkville afterwards so we won't need that food. I'll be out again in a day or so to check with you. So long.'

Three horses moved away and full silence returned. Bannon went to where Bella was standing.

'Governor Mayhew sent me in here,' he said. 'I'm to pass on to you any messages I may have for him. He said you'd get them through.'

'That's why I'm here.' She glanced at him. 'But Jake's death changes everything. It isn't safe here any more, and I reckon to take Cal out of this. I talked it over with Jake when the riders started calling. He wanted me to leave last week but I knew the governor was sending someone in here so I waited for you to show up. But I reckon the bad men have got wise to us. They must know we're passing on information, so it's time to leave.'

Bannon wrinkled his nose at the pungent smell of gunsmoke permeating the room. He looked at Cal Garner, sitting on the floor beside the stove, his knees drawn up, elbows resting on them and his hands supporting his head. He nodded.

'I'll see you into Clarkville tomorrow,' he decided. 'I can get my own messages through to headquarters. The sooner you and Cal are out of here the better. I'll camp outside after we've eaten, although I doubt we'll be bothered again tonight.'

Bella nodded agreement. She cooked the meal and served it, and Bannon sat at the table and ate. There was practically no conversation and what there was was stilted, overshadowed by Jake Garner's death. After the meal Bannon went outside, collected his bedroll, and turned in under the stars, off to the right of the cabin. He lay for a long time, his thoughts meandering, before sleep claimed him, and he was awake again as the sun peered above the eastern horizon, his senses alerted by the sound of rapidly approaching hoofs.

Two riders were coming towards the cabin. Bannon drew his pistol and watched them as they drew nearer, studying details. One man was old, the other much younger. Both were well armed, and approached openly. Bannon waited until they entered the yard and then stood up, his gun hand down at his side. The riders spotted him immediately and turned in his direction. They looked as if they had peaceable intentions but Bannon did not holster his gun.

'Who are you?' demanded the older man. He was small-boned, his face grizzled, his faded blue eyes watchful as he reined in.

'A friend of this family,' Bannon replied. 'What's your business?'

'I'm Pete Larter of the Flying L and this is Bob Hallam, my ranch foreman. We met Sheriff Bixby on the trail and he told us what happened here. Figured to ride in to see if there's anything we can do.'

The cabin door opened at that moment and Bella appeared; rifle in hand. She lowered the weapon when she recognized the callers. Hallam stepped down from his saddle and went to her. Larter slid out of leather and trailed his reins. He looked around, his small features set in grim lines.

'I told Jake only last week that he was asking for trouble,' the rancher mused. 'But he was a stubborn man and nothing short of a bullet would have moved him.'

'He collected one, right between the shoulder-blades,' Bannon observed. 'I plan to take Bella and Cal into town this morning.'

'I'll give them room at my place,' Larter offered immediately, and Bannon saw the girl shake her head.

'I've thought it over during the night,' she said. 'I'm staying here. This place belongs to Cal now, and I'm gonna tend it until he's old enough to look after it himself.'

'Come to Flying L,' Hallam urged. 'We'll take care of you, Bella.'

'My mind is made up and nothing will change it,' she asserted. 'Would you like breakfast before you ride on?'

'When are you gonna bury Jake?' Larter demanded. 'I'd like to be on hand for that. Jake was a good friend, and there is little enough I can do in his memory except see him into his grave.'

'After breakfast,' Bella said. 'Food will be ready in fifteen minutes.'

'We'll do some of the morning chores while we're waiting,' Larter replied.

Bannon went to the barn and fed and watered his horse, afterwards standing with Larter in front of the building, watching the approaches to the little ranch.

'Seems like there is a lot of trouble around here,' Bannon mused.

'Jake was a fool for settling down here. In this part of the country the law is a joke. Bixby makes a big show of riding around hunting the bad men, but obviously he ain't worrying them none or they would have shot him the minute he began to get in their hair. There must be at least one hundred rustlers and outlaws hiding in the Big Bend country, and it would take more than the whole damn passel of Rangers in Texas to root them out. You look like a man who can use that hogleg you're wearing, so where do you fit in around here?'

'Like I said when you rode in, I'm a friend, and I'll look around to try and pick up the trail of the man or men who shot Jake.'

'And if you catch up with them — what then?'

'It'll be my turn to do some shooting,' Bannon replied.

'And we'll have to come round and bury you.' Larter shook his head. 'If you can take any kind of advice then saddle up and leave pronto for other parts. Hemp Parfitt, the outlaw, is running things around here, and him and his bunch don't miss a damn trick. They'll be showing up the minute they get wind of you.'

'I'll bear that in mind,' Bannon replied, 'but I'll take a look around anyway.'

'It'll be your funeral,' Larter said.

They entered the cabin for breakfast, and afterwards buried Jake Garner on a knoll beside the creek. They were standing by the graveside when a stage-coach appeared and stopped beside the cabin. Bella hurried to speak to the shotgun guard, and Bannon saw her pass a letter to the man before the coach resumed its journey. Larter and

Hallam departed for Clarkville, and Bannon turned his thoughts to his job.

Bella set Cal some chores to do. Bannon saddled his black. When he was ready to travel he approached the woman.

'I still think you should pull out,' he said. 'How long do you think the bad men will leave you alone now Garner is dead?'

'My job is here.' She pulled down the brim of the flat-crowned hat she was wearing to shield her eyes from the rising sun. 'I'll be waiting for your messages.'

'I saw you pass a letter to the shotgun guard on the coach. That's the way you contact the governor, huh?'

'It works quite well.' She nodded. 'There's no telling who works undercover for the law. Where are you heading when you leave here?'

'Clarkville, I guess. I'll scout around there and see what I can learn — unless you've got a better idea.'

'Hemp Parfitt's bunch seems to

concentrate in a triangle formed by the towns of Clarkville in the north, Sadilla in the west, and Hainsford off to the south-east of here. I don't know where they have their hideout. Perhaps they play it smart and get together only when they are breaking the law. Bixby never seems to pick up their trail and, as far as I know, he hasn't arrested one outlaw in the time I've been here. He picks up wrongdoers all the time, but only small fry; no one connected with the gang.'

'That figures.' Bannon shielded his eyes with his left hand when he spotted movement on a nearby rise, and his breathing quickened as he made out the figures of three riders approaching.

'We got company,' he observed. 'Call in Cal and get in the storm cellar while I find out who they are.'

'Is it Bixby coming back?' Bella queried. She did not turn around to look at the newcomers but relied on Bannon's keen gaze.

'They're coming in openly, and all I

can really see at the moment is that all three are wearing sombreros.' Bannon flexed the fingers of his right hand. 'The least you can do is hunt cover in the cabin. I need a free hand out here and I don't want you getting in the line of fire.'

'Cal is in the barn. I'll get my rifle and join him.'

Bannon led his horse around the front corner of the cabin and left it standing with trailing reins. He went around to the rear of the cabin, entered it by the back door, and moved to a front window to watch the arrival of the trio, who came in at a canter straight for the cabin. As they approached he studied them. Two were Mexicans, and the third, dressed in Mexican gear, was a blond North American who had the look of a long rider about him; unkempt, bearded, heavily armed — and all three had an intentness in their manner that indicated they were well accustomed to riding the back trails.

They entered the yard and crossed to the cabin, the hoofs of their mounts rattling on the hardpan. Bannon moved into the open doorway, his right hand down at his side, the butt of his pistol touching the inside of his wrist.

'Howdy?' he greeted.

The *Americano* was middle-aged, moon-faced, thick-limbed and stocky; wearing dusty range clothes, scratched leather chaps, well-worn boots, and twin pistols on crossed cartridge belts — the holsters tied down to his thick thighs. He grinned widely, revealing stained, broken teeth. Strands of lank yellow hair showed from under the brim of his wide-brimmed sombrero.

'You're a stranger here,' he remarked.

'And you're a regular visitor, huh?' Bannon countered.

'What's your business?' the hardcase demanded as if Bannon had not spoken. There was a harsh note in his tone that suggested he was accustomed to respect from all whose trail crossed his. The smile on his face was fixed, but did not exude friendliness. His blue eyes were narrowed, glinting with deadly intention.

'Who are you?' Bannon countered. 'Don't get off your horse,' he added as the man began to dismount. 'You haven't been invited down. Just state your business.'

'I'm Dave Hendry, and nobody tells me to stay in my saddle. Where's Jake Garner. I got a message for him.'

'Jake is dead. He was shot in the back yesterday.'

'So where is the woman who lives here?'

'I'm handling the chores. If you have a message for her then spill it and I'll pass it on.'

'It's for her ears only. You're annoying me, mister. Shut your fool mouth and get Bella out here.'

'And if I don't?' Bannon smiled.

The two Mexicans were motionless, hands close to their holstered guns, their eyes intent upon Bannon's big figure, like vultures waiting for a steer to die before feeding upon it. Hostility oozed from them, and Bannon was steeling himself for action when Bella spoke from just inside the cabin.

'What do you want, Hendry?' she demanded. 'Didn't Jake tell you to stay away from here?'

'The stranger tells me Jake is dead,' Hendry replied. 'What's going on? You know we don't like strangers around here.'

'And we don't like two-bit cattle-thieves on our range,' Bella responded. 'Get out of here before I start triggering my rifle. You know I can hit anything I aim at, and right now my sights are lined up on you, Hendry. Go on — pull out, or you'll be wearing two belly-buttons at your funeral.'

Hendry grinned. 'Come on, Bella, show yourself. I got word for you from Mack Jex. He wants you to ride into Clarkville for a visit.'

'Jex ain't a friend,' Bella responded. 'Get outa here or I'll start shooting.'

'Suit yourself, but you know how

Mack gets angry when you don't do like he wants. Come into town with us and hear what Mack has got to say.'

'I'm through talking,' Bella replied. 'You got ten seconds to turn your horse around and start moving out before I work this rifle. I don't want to see you around here again.'

Bannon stood motionless, content to let Bella call the shots. Neither of the two Mexicans had so much as twitched a muscle. Hendry looked Bannon over and nodded.

'I'll know you again, mister,' he said.

Bella's rifle cracked and a string of echoes fled across the yard. Hendry did not flinch as the bullet kicked up dust beside the right hoof of his horse. His grin widened and he pulled on his right-hand rein, turning his horse and moving away across the yard, followed instantly by his two sidekicks. Bannon watched them go with mixed feelings. His instincts were warning that he should have forced a showdown with the trio, but until he had more knowledge of the local situation he could not afford to take the initiative.

When Hendry had moved out of range, Bannon turned to the cabin door, and saw Bella standing just inside the building, her rifle still covering Hendry.

'Sorry about Hendry,' she said, lowering the rifle. 'He runs the rustling side of Mack Jex's crooked business. Jex is in with Hemp Parfitt. He shifts all the rustled stock that Parfitt gathers. Jex has never forgiven me for walking out on him.'

'Have you reported Jex's connection with Parfitt to the governor?'

'Sure, but he won't create trouble for me by taking Jex yet. He'll be picked up when the gang is captured, along with other lesser crooks who don't know they are on the list. You find out where the Parfitt gang can be trapped and taken, and when I get that information to Mayhew the trap will close and this area will be free of the bad men.'

'It's as simple as that, huh?' Bannon's

eyes were narrowed as he watched Hendry and his two associates disappear into the brush along the trail. 'I don't like the idea of leaving you here alone. Hendry might double back after I've pulled out.'

'I can take care of him if he shows again. You'd better head for Clarkville. Ask Sheriff Bixby if he's got any posters on the Parfitt gang. If you don't know what they look like you could pass them in the street and be none the wiser.'

'I've got pictures of Parfitt and his main side-kicks.' Bannon smiled. 'I'll make for Clarkville, and I'll be back soon as I get the deadwood on the gang.'

'Good luck.' Bella's tone remained unemotional.

Bannon nodded and turned away. He fetched his horse from the side of the cabin, mounted, and rode away steadily without looking back, following the trail Hendry had taken. He did not pause when he reached the spot where Hendry and the Mexicans had turned but pushed the powerful black into a mile-eating lope that took him within sight of Clarkville just after noon.

He reined in on a rise and looked down at the stark town. There was a main street, running east to west, and two cross streets, each with a motley collection of buildings straggling along on either side for several blocks. The buildings, built of adobe, were single storey, except for the hotel, which was built of wood and rose above everything else, looking ugly and sticking out like a sore thumb in the bright sunshine. Off to the right, well clear of town, was a cemetery containing a huddle of wooden crosses and gravestones.

Bannon went on down to the main street and reined in to the livery barn.

An old one-armed man appeared from an adjacent office and came limping to where Bannon stood. His whiskered face was wrinkled, his eyes a faded blue. The empty left sleeve of his jacket was pinned up — cuff to shoulder.

'Howdy?' he greeted. 'You look like you've come a far piece.'

'I'm a travelling man,' Bannon replied. 'Take care of the horse. I don't know how long I'll be staying in town but I reckon a dollar will cover it for now.'

He produced a silver dollar and flipped it into the man's ready hand.

'I'm Rudi Hackmeyer,' the ostler said. 'That sure is some hoss, mister.'

'He suits me.' Bannon stripped saddlebags and Winchester from the animal. 'Take care of the rest for me, huh? Is there a good eating-house in town?'

'Try Maisie's Diner, along the street on the right. You can't miss it. Everyone eats there.'

'Thanks.' Bannon went out to the street and looked around. There were numerous saddle horses standing at various hitch racks along the street, and a couple of buckboards were being loaded in front of a general store. A few townsmen were idling in the shade of the buildings, and Bannon wondered what it would be like to have time on his hands with no investigation to make. He kicked through the dust towards the hotel, aware that he attracted stares from those idlers he passed.

Just before he reached the hotel he came across four men standing in front of an office, and a thrill quivered through him when he recognized Dave Hendry and the two Mexicans, who must have ridden hell for leather to reach town ahead of Bannon. Hendry was grinning, but his eyes were cold and watchful.

'Here's the guy I was telling you about, Mack,' Hendry declared to the fourth man. 'He faced me off out at the Garner place, and I reckon it was his presence that gave Bella the nerve to shoot at me.'

Bannon looked at the fourth man. Mack Jex, he surmised, and did not like what he saw. Jex was short and fleshy, dressed in a blue store-suit that was tight around the shoulders. He was wearing a flat-crowned plains hat that sat squarely on his big skull, and his brown eyes glared at Bannon from under the straight brim as if he were looking at a rattlesnake that needed killing. His round face was pale, his nose long with flaring nostrils, and he had a mouth like a rat-trap.

'What's your name, feller?' Jex demanded.

Bannon paused in mid-stride and surveyed the quartet. He did not answer the question, for Jex's tone was insolent.

'I don't need to ask your name.' he responded. 'You're Mack Jex, right? You sent these three out to the Garner place with a message for Bella. I guess you've got her answer now, and she sends an extra message for you. Keep these men away from her. The next time someone from you shows up she'll shoot to kill.'

In the silence that ensued, Bannon clearly heard Hendry's muttered curse, and a tight smile appeared on his lips as he awaited a reaction. Then Jex swore under his breath. His right hand lifted to the shoulder-holster he was wearing under his jacket and came away gripping the pearl-handled butt of a .41 short-barrelled Colt. The muzzle of the weapon had barely begun to swing to cover Bannon when Bannon's pistol cleared leather and he slammed the muzzle against Jex's gun wrist. Jex cried out in pain and his gun flew from his hand to skitter along the dusty ground.

Hendry moved instinctively as Bannon drew, but his gun was still in its holster when he froze because he was looking into the black muzzle of Bannon's pistol.

'You better change your mind pretty damn quick,' Bannon rapped.

The two Mexicans were motionless. Neither had attempted to draw his gun. They gazed at Bannon with pure hatred in their swarthy faces.

Hendry removed his hand from his gun-butt, glaring at Bannon as if trying to stare him to death. Jex was clasping his gun wrist, his face twisted in pain.

'Have you got the message?' Bannon asked coolly, 'Or do I have to make it more forceful? Stay away from the Garner place and don't interfere with Bella again. If you ignore this warning I'll gutshoot you and everyone you send to pester Bella. Now you'd better disarm yourselves, one at a time, just in case of accidents.'

Hendry moved first. He lifted his pistol from its holster with forefinger and thumb and dropped it into the dust before raising both hands shoulder high. The grin was gone from his face now, and hatred shone in his blue eyes.

'OK, you heard me,' Bannon said to the two Mexicans. 'Get rid of your hardware now.'

The two men moved in unison, both reaching for their holstered guns, and they were fast, their bronzed hands dipping swiftly and coming up filled with gun metal. Bannon's teeth clicked together as he fired, triggering his deadly gun twice in rapid succession. Shots crashed out, throwing harsh echoes across the silent town, and both Mexicans pitched into the dust, their guns spilling from suddenly nerveless hands.

Hendry took advantage of the shooting. His face was contorted by desperation as his right hand dipped down to the back of his neck with the speed of a striking rattler to reappear gripping a long-bladed skinning-knife. His arm went back for power to throw the weapon, and Bannon fired again, aiming for Hendry's right shoulder. The thunder-clap of the shot chased away into the distance as Hendry dropped the knife and spun half-around to fall against Jex and thence to the ground.

Bannon exhaled sharply to rid his lungs of flaring gun-smoke. His eyes were narrowed; his gun poised for more trouble, and he was aware that he had made a good start in his new assignment for the law.

3

Bannon leaned his Winchester against a wall as he gazed at the scene of violence confronting him. The two Mexicans were inert, dead, each with a half-inch chunk of lead embedded in his heart. Hendry was sprawled on the ground with his back against the front wall of the office, his left hand pressed against the bloodstain showing on his right shoulder. Mack Jex was leaning back against the same wall, still gripping his right wrist, his eyes filled with shock and disbelief showing on his fleshy features. Gun echoes faded slowly into the distance. Bannon reloaded his pistol, his narrowed eyes taking in his surroundings. Men were beginning to appear on the street, attracted by the shooting.

Sheriff Bixby emerged from the doorway of the hotel, closely followed by the two deputies who had accompanied him at Jake Garner's ranch, and they were the first to reach the scene. The old lawman, his law badge glinting in the sunlight, glanced cursorily at the dead Mexicans, bent to pick up Hendry's discarded pistol, and then turned to confront Jex.

'It looks like you bit off more than you could chew this time, Mack,' Bixby said, before glancing at Bannon, who remained motionless, his pistol down at his side. 'And it didn't take you long to rub someone up the wrong way, huh? No need for me to ask who started it. Hendry has been asking for trouble for a long time. It's a pity you didn't kill him, mister. That's the way he's gonna get it one of these days, and he sure pushes for trouble.'

'This stranger attacked us without warning,' Jex said harshly. 'Throw him in jail, Bixby, and lose the key.'

'Don't try to tell me my job.' Bixby bristled and his eyes blazed. 'So what happened here? Who started it?'

'I just told you — the stranger did,' Jex insisted.

'OK, we'll do it the hard way.' Bixby sighed. 'Come along to my office and we'll sort it out there.' He glanced at his deputies. 'Ike, fetch Doc Keaton. I'll leave Hendry here — don't want him dribbling blood all over the office, and after you've fetched the doc, cut along to Allen's office and tell him there are a couple of stiffs to be handled. Let's get this place cleaned up pronto.'

Ike Marsden went off along the street. Bixby took Jex by an elbow and began to propel him towards the jail. He glanced at Bannon in passing. 'You better come along. I'll need your side of this.'

Bannon holstered his pistol and picked up his rifle. The crowd followed as Bixby led his prisoner to the jail. Joe Renton, the other deputy, walked at Bannon's side. They entered the law office and Renton slammed the door on the gathering townsfolk.

'I need the doc,' Jex complained. 'I've

got a broken wrist.'

'One of these days you'll get a broken neck,' Bixby said unsympathetically. 'I've been keeping a rope handy for that day. Sit down and shut up. You'll have a chance to talk when I get around to you, and you better come up with the truth.' He eyed Bannon for a moment. 'What have you got to say about this, mister? You ride into my town, kill a couple of men, and raise all kinds of a ruckus, but you don't look like a troublemaker, so what gives?'

Bannon explained the sequence of events and Bixby nodded, his narrowed eyes gleaming.

'Sounds like a lover's quarrel between Bella and Jex that got out of hand, and you got dragged into it,' he surmised. 'OK. Let it be a warning to you. Don't get caught up in local affairs. You can go now. Jex and Hendry will be fined for disturbing the peace, and that had better be an end of it. If you ain't got any business in these parts, mister, then you'd be wise to shake the dust of this town off your boots and head for other pastures.'

Bannon frowned and departed, surprised by Bixby's methods of handling the law. He pushed through the crowd outside the office and walked along to the hotel, his keen gaze taking note of his surroundings. Some of the townsfolk followed him at a respectful distance and stood at the door of the hotel while he rented a room. He collected a key, ascended the stairs to the first floor and, as soon as he had deposited his gear and rifle in the room, relocked the door and went back down to the street.

Feeling the need of a drink, he entered the nearest saloon, and found Hendry inside, lying on a long table, being treated by the doctor, a short, thin man with a careworn face and untidy grey hair. Hendry was bare-chested, and several men were watching the doctor's ministrations. Bannon went to the bar and ordered a drink. He took stock of his surroundings, and noted the men who were present.

He had images in his mind of the outlaws who formed the nucleus of the Parfitt gang, and hoped to spot one of them and follow him to the hideout of the rest of the gang. Such an event would save him much of the groundwork that had to be done, but he suspected that nothing would go right for him in this particular case and he would have to use a great deal of patience to dig up clues to the whereabouts of the gang.

The bartender slid a tall glass of foaming beer along the bar top to where Bannon was standing, and then came to collect his money. He was tall and thin, with receding black hair, and his brown eyes were sharp and alert as he picked up the silver dollar Bannon slapped on the bar.

'Say, don't I know you from somewhere?' the 'tender demanded.

Bannon shook his head. 'I've never been this way before, but I'm looking for a riding job so if you got any ideas on that subject I'll be pleased to hear them. You look like a man who has knowledge of local affairs. Is there anything doing in the cattle business?'

'Customers do come in and talk,' the 'tender agreed. 'I'm Al Hilliard. I own this place. You're the man who did the shooting outside a few minutes ago, huh? You must be pretty slick with your gun and should have no trouble finding a job.'

'I'm looking for a riding job,' Bannon insisted, 'not gun-work.'

'You put a slug through Dave Hendry so you'll have plenty to do to stay alive when Hendry can pick up a gun again. His boss, Mack Jex, runs a tough crew around here. Jex owns the M Bar J ranch, and has his finger in several business affairs around the county — most of them crooked. He's the man you should approach about a job, but after what you did to Hendry I reckon Jex will probably have you run out of town or killed. He might have forgiven you for nailing Hendry, but the two

Mexes you killed were the top men who handled his crooked interests across the border in Mexico. That is something he won't forgive.'

Bannon took a swig of beer and glanced around the big room. It was unfortunate that he had crossed Hendry's trail, but Bella had told him that Jex was involved in rustling, which was a lead he could not afford to overlook.

'Mind you,' Hilliard continued, 'you could do worse than talk to Colonel Maddock. He owns the Sabre outfit north of here, and runs his spread like he was still in the army. That's him at the corner table over there with his foreman, Al Piercey. If you can rub along with Piercey then you could have yourself a good job.'

Bannon glanced around, his narrowed gaze taking in the two men seated at a corner table. There was a bottle of whiskey and two glasses on the table between them. The colonel was about sixty and of medium build, lean and dried up, but showing rawhide strength. There was no flesh on his face — the leathery skin was stretched tightly over his prominent cheekbones. His dark eyes were far-seeing, seemingly made of glass, and his thin lips displayed the predatory eagerness of a ravenous timber-wolf. He was dressed in a good quality dark-blue store-suit; a white shirt and a black string tie. A flat-brimmed plains hat was pushed back off his forehead revealing grey hair. There was a gun on his right thigh and highly polished riding-boots on his feet.

Al Piercey was heavily built, powerful, with broad shoulders and muscular arms. He was in his early forties. His fleshy face was rounded, clean shaven, and he had a thick shock of black hair. He was dressed in range clothes and armed with a holstered pistol on his right hip.

Both men were looking at Bannon as he surveyed them, and a silence ensued that seemed to have undertones of hostility. Bannon straightened and walked across to their table, the rowels on his spurs tinkling musically with each step he took. He halted a couple of feet from the table, his gaze intent upon Maddock, who regarded him silently. As Bannon moistened his lips to speak Piercey forestalled him.

'We don't hire saddle tramps,' the foreman grated in a voice that sounded as though it started from his dusty boots.

Bannon remained silent, considering Piercey's insolence, and tension seeped into the atmosphere. Piercey smiled, his eyes alight with brutal pleasure as he awaited Bannon's reaction to his words.

'I guess it takes one to recognize another.' Bannon's voice sounded like steel rasping against gravel, 'and you've got all the give-away signs, mister. You don't have any sense either, picking on a stranger.'

Piercey's expression changed instantly and he started to his feet, overturning his chair in the process. He swung to face Bannon, who threw a solid right-hand punch that landed his clenched fist against Piercey's jaw. Piercey tried to evade the blow but was too slow, and he went backwards for several feet on his heels, trying desperately to maintain his balance until the shock of the blow got through to his senses and his balance failed. His legs suddenly lost their strength and he dropped to the floor where he lay gasping.

'You impress me.' Colonel Maddock smiled easily, his gaze upon his hapless foreman. 'Piercey always braces the men who come seeking employment at Sabre, and this is the first time I've seen him discomfited. I'm a good judge of men, but I must confess there's something about you that doesn't add up. You're not what you seem. Perhaps you're trying too hard to cover up your real intentions. My first impression of you is unfavourable so I cannot use you, and my advice to you is ride for other parts. If you stay around here, Piercey will try to kill you for what you've done to his reputation, and I have a sneaking feeling you can beat him with a pistol and I can't afford to lose him. You won't find work around here, so cut your losses and pull out.'

Bannon was watching Piercey intently, his gunhand down at his side. 'I wasn't looking for trouble,' he said quietly. 'All I want is a job.'

Piercey began to get to his feet, shaking his head to clear his senses. A trickle of blood was showing at a corner of his set mouth. He took a step towards Bannon, his hands clenching into fists.

'Cut it out, Piercey,' Maddock said harshly, getting to his feet. 'You'll be wasting your time. You haven't got the beating of him in you, and if you can't see that then you're a fool. Come along. We have an appointment elsewhere.'

Piercey wiped his mouth on the back of his hand. 'I'll see you again, mister,' he growled 'and the next time it'll be through gunsmoke. You've started something you won't ever get to finish.'

'Talk is cheap,' Bannon responded.

He watched the colonel head for

the batwings. Piercey followed his employer, his thick shoulders stiff, his steps jerky and irregular. The batwings swung behind the pair, and Bannon listened to their footsteps receding outside. He walked back to the bar. Hilliard was standing motionless with shock showing plainly on his face.

'Well whaddya make of that?' the 'tender remarked, shaking his head. 'I've heard that Piercey shakes down every rider who tries for work with Sabre, but he sure came unstuck with you. For someone who wants to get a job around here, you have a strange way of treating prospective employers. You've put yourself in bad with Jex, and now you've done the same with Colonel Maddock.'

'I didn't have any choice.' Bannon smiled. 'I guess I'll have to spin my loop wider. There must be other ranchers around who could use a top hand.'

'Well, good luck. You're sure gonna need it. It'll be interesting to watch your progress.'

'Thanks.' Bannon finished his beer and departed. He subjected the street to a close scrutiny before moving along to the eating-house, where a big sign over its doorway bore the legend: MAISIE'S DINER. He entered, sat at a corner table, and ordered a meal from a waitress. He had no doubts that his present assignment would prove to be the toughest he had ever embarked on.

The diner was busy. Bannon had to wait some minutes before his meal arrived, and he had barely begun to eat when a youth approached his table.

'Mind if I sit down, mister?' he asked. 'This place is crowded today — too many strangers in town. Must be something bad cooking.'

'Help yourself,' Bannon replied. 'I'm a stranger here but I'm not involved in anything.' He noticed the youth's hesitancy as he sat down. 'You live in town, I reckon.'

'Sure thing! And wish I didn't. Clarkville is a one-horse town. If you don't work for Mack Jex or Colonel

Maddock then you've got nothing.'

'Who do you work for?' Bannon's gaze rested on the youth's pimply face.

'Rudi Hackmeyer, the stableman. I'm Pete Lambert. My pa was the sheriff here until the outlaws killed him two years ago and put Bixby in as their man. I was hoping to become a deputy sheriff, but with Pa dead I don't have a chance. I've got a message for you, from Hackmeyer. A man rode into the stable a few minutes ago asking questions about someone he was looking for. He showed Hackmeyer a handbill with your face on it. You're wanted by the Texas Rangers, and there's a price of two thousand dollars on your head — dead or alive. Hackmeyer don't talk about any of his customers to nobody, so he kept his lip buttoned. The man went along to the sheriff's office and Hackmeyer sent me to warn you.'

Bannon did not stop eating while Lambert was talking, and showed no outward sign of agitation at the news.

'What did the guy look like?' he asked.

'Big man — like a bear — had a fleshy face covered in ginger whiskers and eyes he might have stolen from a hog. Bounty hunter, Hackmeyer called him. He looks like a lot of trouble.'

'Thanks for warning me.' Bannon produced a silver dollar and flipped it across the table. 'Go back to the barn and saddle my horse. I'll be along shortly.'

'Hackmeyer was saddling up for you as I left the stable.'

'Good. Now you better get out of here.'

Lambert got to his feet and departed in a hurry. Bannon continued with his meal, his thoughts busy. From the description Lambert had given of the bounty hunter, he guessed the man was Tom Arbuck. Their trails had crossed in the past and Bannon had narrowly escaped with his life. He wondered how Arbuck had got on his trail again.

He finished his meal, paid his bill, and then followed the waitress through to the kitchen, aiming to leave by the back door. A big, middle-aged woman was supervising the kitchen, and she approached him quickly, wiping her hands on a cloth.

'The kitchen is off limits,' she said.

'I'm leaving by the back door.' Bannon smiled disarmingly. 'Thanks for the meal. I've never tasted better.'

'I'm Maisie,' she said. 'Come again, but bear in mind that I like my customers to use the front door.'

Bannon touched the brim of his hat in acknowledgement and continued. He paused in the doorway and looked around the back lots before leaving his cover, and then made for the rear of the jail, reaching its cover without incident.

There was a back door, which was locked. Bannon entered the alley at the side of the building and walked to the street end. He glanced around the street, which seemed peaceful, and noted a big bay horse hitched to the rail in front of the law office — the animal Tom Arbuck usually rode. He waited with his right hand down at his side, his fingers curled ready to grasp the butt of his gun.

From his position he could see the alley opposite the diner, and caught a glimpse of two men standing just inside the mouth of the alley, apparently watching the front door of the diner. One of them was holding a double-barrelled shotgun. Bannon firmed his lips at the signs, and realized that he had narrowly escaped being trapped in the eating-house. He backed away from the street and retraced his steps along the alley. Checking the back lots, he spotted two Mexicans to his left, taking up positions to cover the rear door of the diner.

Bannon decided it was time to pull out. Clarkville was too hot for him at the moment. He would have to withdraw and rethink his approach. He glanced back over his shoulder to check the street end of the alley and saw a man moving into the alley mouth. He eased out of the alley and stood with his back to the building on his right, his keen gaze flitting around, aware that he had no option but to head for the stable and ride out for safer pastures. He had grabbed a wildcat by the tail and it was time to let go.

He stayed close to the buildings and walked towards the stable, his shoulders hunched in anticipation of shots being directed at him from behind, but the two Mexicans outside the diner were evidently concentrating on what they were doing and failed to spot his movement. He breathed more easily when he reached the corral at the back of the stable, and sneaked into the gloomy barn.

A smacking sound as of a wet cloth striking a rock echoed through the stable, Bannon paused and looked around. It sounded as if Hackmeyer was doing his laundry in the horse-trough, but the insistent noise was coming from the small office. Bannon palmed his Colt and stalked forward, a frown creasing his forehead, He looked in through the open doorway of the office and saw Pete Lambert stretched out on the floor with blood on his face. Two men were standing over Hackmeyer, who was behind his desk. One of them was beating the ostler with a leather belt. Bloody welts were showing on the stableman's face.

Bannon stepped into the office, his pistol swinging. He struck the man wielding the belt and felled him with a blow to the back of his neck. The second man swung round, reaching for his holstered gun. Bannon caught him with a backhanded blow that laid his pistol barrel against the man's forehead and dropped him to his knees. Hackmeyer was dazed, his craggy face bruised and bleeding. He gazed at Bannon with eyes devoid of expression.

'Who are these men?' Bannon demanded.

Hackmeyer gulped and straightened, leaning back in his chair. Bannon bent over the men he had felled and disarmed them, throwing their weapons into the barn.

'They rode in with Arbuck, the

bounty hunter,' Hackmeyer gasped. 'They didn't believe me when I said I didn't know where you were. Is Pete OK?'

Bannon checked the supine Lambert. He nodded.

'He'll be OK. Face is bruised, that's all. I'll hogtie these two before I face Arbuck.'

'You won't find him alone now,' Hackmeyer said. 'He went to the jail to talk to Bixby. You can't fight the whole bunch of them. Bixby is crooked, and he'll want a cut of the reward on your head.'

'He won't get it.' Bannon shook his head. 'Arbuck never split a reward in his life. I don't know what he's doing with these two — maybe he's got too old to work alone.'

'You'd do better to ride out and come back later, if you've got business around here,' Hackmeyer advised.

Bannon took a coil of rope off a hook in the back wall and bound the two hardcases together. Hackmeyer pushed himself to his feet and staggered around the desk. His leathery face was bruised and his right hand was shaking, but he picked up a shotgun that was leaning in a corner and checked its loads. He looked resolute, but he staggered as he stood over his attackers.

'These two can go to jail for assault,' he declared. 'Bixby might be crooked, but he has to deal some semblance of the law to justify his position. I'll take them along to the law office soon as they can get up and walk. I saddled your horse. It's in the corral out back.'

'Thanks, but if I don't face down Tom Arbuck right now he'll be making a try for me soon as he's got an edge.'

Hackmeyer fetched water in a bucket and sprinkled it on Pete Lambert's upturned face. The youth came to his senses and Bannon helped him to his feet.

'When you feel able to, go along to the sheriff's office and tell Arbuck you've seen me riding out of town in the direction of Sadilla,' Bannon said.

'I'll stay here and watch for Arbuck to leave.'

'Then you better get under cover before these two hardcases can set eyes on you,' Hackmeyer warned.

'I wanta be on hand to see that Arbuck doesn't harm you before he leaves,' Bannon said. 'He's a bad man to cross, and he may reckon you've stepped over the line to help me.'

'Get under cover now,' Hackmeyer insisted. 'Those two are coming round.'

A noise at the door of the office sent Bannon whirling around, his right hand flashing to his holstered gun. He saw a massive figure filling the doorway and recognized Tom Arbuck. The bounty hunter took in the scene before him and reached for his pistol. Bannon drew fast and cocked his gun as it levelled. Then all hell broke loose. Arbuck moved incredibly fast for a man of his size, throwing himself out of the doorway and into cover, his pistol blasting rapidly, filling the barn with gun thunder.

Bannon dropped to one knee as he triggered his Colt. He sprang up when Arbuck stopped shooting, dived out through the office doorway, and sent a shot at Arbuck's fast-disappearing figure as the big man made a hasty retreat from the barn. Moving quickly, Bannon went in pursuit, all else forgotten in his desire to remove the threat that Arbuck posed.

4

Echoes of the shooting were fading over the town as Bannon reached the street. He saw Arbuck to his left, dropping into cover behind a wagon loaded high with straw, and fired a shot which clipped the brim of the bounty hunter's hat. Arbuck replied with two quick, accurate shots, and Bannon heard the slugs boring through the wall of the barn beside his head.

Movement to the right attracted Bannon's attention and he eased back into the doorway of the barn, his pistol levelled. He saw Sheriff Bixby and his two deputies advancing from the cover of the last of the buildings on the street, kicking through the dust, their pistols drawn. Bixby paused when he was within shouting distance and his deputies ranged up on either side of him.

'Arbuck, come out with your hands

up,' Bixby ordered. 'I warned you against trying anything inside town limits. Put up your gun and show yourself. You in the barn, hold your fire.'

Bannon did not reply. He could see the brim of Arbuck's hat showing at one end of the wagon and covered it. Surprise filled him when Arbuck stepped into view with his deadly pistol in its holster. The bounty hunter halted and stood facing the door of the barn, his feet planted solidly in the dust and his right hand ready to grasp the butt of his gun.

'Now you, stranger,' Bixby called. 'Arbuck says you're an outlaw. Well, there'll be no trouble in this town so come out and we'll get to the bottom of this.'

Bannon turned on his heel and went quickly to the big rear door. His black horse was standing in the corral, saddled and ready to travel, and he tightened the cinch, stepped up into the leather, and touched spurs to the animal's flanks. He left Clarkville at a canter, his head turned to watch his back trail. He saw Pete Lambert appear briefly in the doorway of the barn. The youth waved in Bannon's direction, and Bannon frowned as he pushed the horse into a mile-eating lope.

He did not doubt that Arbuck would take up his trail as soon as he got clear of Bixby. The bounty hunter was a hard-bitten killer who had no scruples when it came to tracking down an outlaw with a price on his head. Bannon had no wish to kill the man, whose violent and precarious way of life did much to decrease the odds against more regular law dealers, but he was aware that Arbuck never relinquished the trail of a bad man once he had taken up the challenge, and it was on the cards that he would reappear on the scene just when Bannon could least afford a diversion from his main chore.

He rode the trail towards Sadilla, intent on getting to grips with his job. Clarkville had barely faded into his back trail when he became aware of being followed. He saw nothing, but a prickling sensation along his spine alerted him and he pushed the black into greater effort. When he reached a long stretch of fairly level ground he crossed it at a gallop and crossed a ridge that soon covered him from anyone following. He reined up in deep cover, snatched his Winchester from its boot, and returned to the crest to drop flat and observe his back trail.

Minutes passed and he saw nothing. His keen eyes searched the surrounding skyline, looking for furtive movement and the glint of sunlight on metal, but there was nothing to be seen. His instinct told him to be on his way, but he lingered, certain that someone was on his back trail.

Eventually he remounted and set off again, but after travelling one hundred yards he swung off the trail and circled back two miles, aiming to cut his own trail back beyond the spot where he had sensed he was being followed. When he regained the trail he saw his own sign, plus two sets of fresh tracks.

He sat his horse, studying the tracks, and followed them to where they had turned off and headed west. He dismounted and checked them more closely, noting characteristics about them which would enable him to recognize them again. He rode on, following the tracks, wanting to find out who was interested in his movements. He was intrigued when he found two more sets of tracks joining the ones he was following. He reined in to consider them.

Bannon sat for a long time looking at the tracks before continuing to follow them. The riders were moving at a fair clip and he pushed the black into a faster gait. After two hours of riding he came to a ridge from where he sat peering down at a large ranch head-quarters — the tracks he had been following had veered off to the left to circle the ranch. He took his field glasses from his saddle-bag and focused them on the distant scene. There were a number of men standing on the porch of the large house, and one of the first he picked out with the glasses was Al Piercey, Colonel Maddock's foreman.

So this was Sabre, the colonel's cattle spread. Bannon swung his glasses and counted more than twenty men on the ranch. Several were standing by one of the two large corrals, another two were in the doorway of the barn, and some were preparing to ride out. The ranch was a hive of activity, but none of it seemed normal. At this time of the morning ranch hands were usually out tending the herds. Bannon dismounted, led his horse into cover, and returned to the ridge on foot to belly down and watch proceedings.

A lone rider crossed the Sabre yard and loped along the faint trail that led to Clarkville. Bannon focused on the figure and frowned when he saw it was a pretty girl of about twenty years old. He watched her progress until she had passed his position at a distance of a hundred yards to disappear beyond a ridge, then returned his attention to the ranch. More than half the men in the yard were mounted now and heading out. They formed a compact group and rode like a troop of cavalry, hitting a fast canter and disappearing over a ridge to the north.

A shot hammered suddenly and echoes fled across the range. Bannon's head turned quickly and he peered into the direction the girl had taken. It sounded as if she had found trouble. He sprang up and ran to the black, swung into the saddle and urged the animal into movement, his rifle in his right hand. The black covered the ground quickly, and moments later Bannon spotted a riderless horse coming towards him, stirrups flying as it headed back to the ranch.

The significance of the shot struck Bannon hard. Had the girl been shot? He spurred the black into a full gallop, and its speeding hoofs rattled the hard trail. Bannon's gaze studied the ground.

Tracks were easy to spot in the thick dust, and he recognized two sets as being similar to those he had found on his back trail. He followed them, hoping the girl was safe.

He came eventually to where the tracks of two other horses converged on the trail from the right, and sped on, following four sets of tracks. These halted within the next fifty yards, and Bannon, adept at reading sign, saw where the girl's horse had wheeled and started back to the ranch. The ground was trampled, and he saw spots of blood in the dust. Two riders had headed back in the direction of Clarkville, and he picked up the tracks of the pair of riders who had turned to the west. He set out after them, for one of the horses was carrying double, judging by the depth of its tracks.

Bannon wondered about the girl. She must be still alive or the men would not be taking her away. He hammered up a long rise and paused on the crest to look around, his eyes narrowing against the sunlight when he spotted two riders ahead, in the act of moving into a narrow draw. One of the men had the girl across his saddle. Bannon waited until they had disappeared from view before following.

The draw was cut into a long rise in the ground, and Bannon rode to one side, travelling faster on the open range. He could see where the draw flattened out higher up, and rode fast to get to the exit before the riders could emerge. He was sitting his horse, ready and waiting, pistol in hand, when the man carrying the girl rode out of the draw. The rider was hampered by the girl, but made an instant play for his holstered pistol despite being covered by Bannon's gun. The second rider appeared behind the first, and swung his horse immediately to ride back into the draw.

Bannon jumped his horse forward to get alongside the rider with the girl, his big pistol swinging. The man pushed the girl to the ground, and finished his draw, bringing his Colt up out of his holster. Bannon slammed his barrel against the man's wrist and the pistol dropped to the ground. The man gave up then, raising his hands in token of surrender.

The girl was moving, Bannon noted. He motioned for the rider to dismount. The second man was crashing back down the draw to get away, and Bannon let him go. He dismounted, covering his prisoner with his gun, and made the man lie spread-eagled on the ground. Keeping an eye on him, Bannon went to the girl's side and examined her, fearing that she had been shot, but she had apparently injured herself in falling from her horse, for there was a bruise on her right cheek and blood on her forehead.

Bannon fetched his canteen from the black and sprinkled water on the girl's face. Her eyes flickered, then opened, and she looked around dazedly. Bannon sat back on his heels and watched her. There was no fear in her eyes when she looked at him.

'You'll rue the day you stopped me,' she asserted. 'My grandfather will string you up to the nearest tree when he learns about this.'

'Not me, I hope,' Bannon said. 'I rescued you from the two men who grabbed you. One of them is stretched out over there. I was watching Sabre when you left, then I heard a shot and saw your horse running back to the ranch without you. I came to look for you, saw two men carrying you off and ambushed them right here. So tell me what happened. You came out of the Sabre ranch so I assume you're related to Colonel Maddock.'

'I'm Sarah Maddock. The colonel is my grandfather. I'm sorry if I'm wrong about you. All I can remember is two men stopping me on the trail, and one of them fired a shot in the air when I attempted to flee. My horse reared and threw me and I struck my head.'

'Do you know this man?' Bannon ordered his prisoner to rise and the man got to his feet.

Sarah gazed at her assailant, then nodded slowly. 'Yes. His name is Carter. He works for Mack Jex.'

'I've met Jex.' Bannon's eyes gleamed with sudden interest. 'I had a run-in with Dave Hendry in town and had to put a slug through his shoulder. So why is Jex interested in grabbing you off the range?'

'He hates my grandfather. They were business rivals for years. I think Jex swindled Grandfather out of some range a long time ago, and Grandfather is not the type of man to forget a thing like that.'

Sarah groaned and put a hand to her head. Bannon slid an arm around her slender shoulders to support her as she staggered.

'I'd better get you back to the ranch,' he said. 'Do you think you can sit a saddle?'

'I'll be all right.' She nodded. 'What will you do with Carter?'

'You can ride his horse. I know what he looks like so I can get to him any

83

time, unless he leaves the county.' He waved his pistol at Carter. 'Get out of here,' he ordered. 'I'll catch up with you later, and if I don't then I'm sure the Sabre outfit will wanta talk to you when they learn what you've done. I guess the best thing you can do is slope out of the county.'

Carter turned to his horse and Bannon stopped him.

'You can pick up your bronc later from the colonel,' he said with a grin. 'Right now you'll have to walk back to town, so get moving before I change my mind and put a slug through you.'

Carter turned and almost ran into the draw. Bannon helped the girl into the saddle of Carter's horse, gathered up his reins and mounted, and they set off back towards Sabre. They had barely covered a quarter of the distance when five riders appeared on the nearest ridge and came at a gallop towards them. Bannon recognized Colonel Maddock in the lead, and kept his hand away from his gun as the riders came up and surrounded them.

'Are you all right, Sarah?' Maddock demanded. 'We heard a shot along the trail, and your horse came back to the ranch alone. There's blood on your forehead. What happened?'

Bannon sat motionless while Sarah explained the incident, and Maddock ordered two of his men to enter the draw and search for the riders. His glasslike eyes glittered as he looked at Bannon.

'I'm beholden to you for going to Sarah's aid,' he said. 'But what were you doing spying on Sabre?'

Bannon smiled. 'Not spying, Colonel. I learned in town that your spread is the largest in the county so I reckoned to try you again for a job.'

'After your run-in with my foreman?' Maddock smiled grimly. 'You must need a job pretty bad.'

'I didn't come off second best, remember,' Bannon reminded him.

Maddock nodded. 'OK. I'll give you a job. You look like you can handle what

I have in mind. Ride to Sabre with us.'

Sarah rode beside her grandfather with Bannon following them closely, and the remaining two Sabre riders brought up the rear. They cantered steadily back to Sabre headquarters and rode into the yard. Bannon's keen gaze noted several of Maddock's men around the yard, crouching in defensive positions and holding rifles at the ready.

'Expecting trouble, Colonel?' Bannon asked as they dismounted at the porch of the house.

'Not expecting it, just ready should it come,' Maddock replied. 'It's my military training, I guess. We've had trouble in the past, and I can't believe it won't happen again.'

Al Piercey emerged from the house at that moment and paused on the porch, his eyes narrowing as he gazed at Bannon.

'What's he doin' here?' he demanded truculently. 'I thought we decided to keep him out.'

'He saved Sarah from a couple of

Jex's hardcases,' Maddock replied, 'so I reckon I can use him. Are you questioning my decisions again, Piercey? Why aren't you out with Mason and his party?'

'Mason can handle that chore without me breathing down his neck.' Piercey came to the edge of the porch and glared at Bannon. 'What are you after around here, mister? You ain't an ordinary line rider.'

'What are you scared of?' Bannon countered. 'You talk like a man who's got something to hide.'

'I'm scared of nothing — man or beast.' Piercey stepped down off the porch, shrugging his shoulders and clenching his big hands into fists.

'You tried that already and came off second best,' Bannon observed, deliberately goading the big ramrod.

'Lay off,' Maddock rapped. 'I'll tell you what you can do right now, Al, and that's fire Joe Parmalee. He's supposed to be escorting Sarah every minute she's off the ranch, so what was he doing when she rode out alone this morning and found trouble?'

'Joe's gone with Mason. He can't be in two places at once.'

'And you figured Mason's chore was more important than my granddaughter's life, huh?' Maddock's voice sharpened with irritation. 'Just do like I say, Al, or you'll be looking for another job.'

Piercey bristled, his temper flaring, but he held himself in and shook his head. He turned abruptly and headed for the corral, brushing Bannon's shoulder in passing. Bannon turned to keep the ramrod under observation.

'One of these days I will fire that galoot,' Maddock said testily. 'Come into the house — say, what's your name? Who in Sam Hill are you?'

'I'm Kelly.'

'Just Kelly?' Maddock persisted. 'Is that your given or your family name?'

'I've never been called anything but Kelly,' Bannon replied, 'and that's all I answer to.'

'OK. Then Kelly it is. Come into my study and we'll have a chat. Sarah, bring us some coffee. You look like you could do with something after your experience.'

'No thanks,' the girl replied as they entered the house 'I'll get your coffee, and then I shall want to go into Clarkville.'

Bannon followed Maddock along a passage and entered the study behind the colonel while Sarah went on to the kitchen at the rear of the house.

'Sit down, Kelly.' Maddock moved to a padded leather seat behind an ornate desk situated by a large window which gave a view of the front yard and the bunkhouse. He sat down, rested his elbows on the desk, and gazed at Bannon for some moments without speaking. Bannon returned the stare with interest, his eyes unwavering.

'I never know what is going to happen next around here,' Maddock said at length. 'Most of the trouble I can handle, but my granddaughter is another matter, and I can't afford to take any chances with her life. There have been indications before today that someone plans to use her as a lever against me. I've been closing my mind to the facts, but what happened this morning has opened my eyes. I need a good man to guard Sarah and keep trouble from her, and you stepped into the picture and proved you're up to the chore. So what do you say? Will you ride herd on her? You'll draw gun wages, because I expect you to shoot to kill to ensure her safety.'

'I need a job, and if guarding your granddaughter is all you've got to offer then I'll take it,' Bannon replied without hesitation.

'Then start right away. Become Sarah's shadow and watch out for her.'

'Why does Jex want to get at you through your granddaughter?'

Maddock's glasslike gaze sharpened and his teeth clicked together. 'I'll be paying Jex a visit shortly, so that side of it needn't interest you. Just watch Sarah and keep trouble from her; no questions asked. You'll sleep in the house

— I'll get Sarah to prepare a room for you. Don't let her out of your sight if she leaves the ranch.'

'It seems straightforward enough.' Bannon nodded. 'I can handle that with no trouble at all.'

The door opened and Sarah entered bearing a tray. She smiled at Bannon as she handed him a cup of coffee.

'I haven't thanked you for saving me this morning,' she said in a low voice. 'It was very frightening to be stopped and grabbed like that.' She glanced at Maddock. 'What do you suppose was behind it, Grandfather?'

'I'm working on that,' Maddock said tersely. 'Don't worry your head about it, Sarah. I've engaged Kelly to guard you. In future you don't leave the ranch without him. Is that clear? I don't need to worry about you when you're out of my sight. I know you haven't taken any of my warnings seriously before today, but after what's happened you should be worried, and I hope you'll be more sensible in future.'

'I'll do like you say,' she responded. She made to depart but paused in the doorway and looked back at Bannon. 'Will you be ready to escort me to town in about thirty minutes?' she asked.

'I'll be standing by,' he replied.

She smiled again and closed the door. Bannon was impressed by her beauty.

'I need to know a bit about her,' he said. 'Is she courting? Is there anyone I can permit to get close to her?'

'You'll have to ask her about her personal life.' Maddock smiled. 'I don't pry into her affairs. There was a man who showed an interest in her some time ago, but he turned out to be unsuitable and I haven't seen her with anyone lately. She doesn't mention that side of her life to me these days. I have always given her a free rein, and so far she's done nothing to worry me.'

'Maybe you should restrict her movements for a spell,' Bannon suggested.

'You try that and see how far you

get.' Maddock nodded. 'I shall be interested to see how you make out.'

Bannon drank his coffee. Maddock arose from the desk and stood before the window, staring out across the yard. Bannon could see Al Piercey over by the bunkhouse. The ramrod was talking to one of the men, waving his arms and shaking his head. Bannon would have given a lot to know what the big foreman was saying.

'I've heard there's a lot of lawlessness around here,' Bannon said conversationally. 'When I met Bixby at Jake Garner's place he said he had been trailing four bank robbers. I found Jake Garner lying dead on his stoop — he'd been murdered — shot in the back.'

'And you killed two of Jex's Mexican friends and plugged Dave Hendry through the shoulder.' Maddock turned his back to the window and subjected Bannon to a level glance. 'That's why I've got doubts about you. I think you are more than you're admitting to. Are you working for the law?'

Bannon shook his head and smiled. 'You couldn't be further from the truth,' he said. 'But whatever I am, I'll guard your granddaughter with my life, if necessary. She'll be safe with me.'

Maddock nodded. 'That's all I need to know about you,' he said.

'I'd better take care of my horse if I'm to ride back to town shortly.'

Bannon turned to the door, and as he opened it to depart he heard the sound of glass shattering. Swinging around to face Maddock again, he saw the rancher crumpling to the floor. A windowpane beyond Maddock was broken, and the sound of a distant shot came faintly to Bannon's keen ears.

For a split second Bannon was transfixed by shock, then he was galvanized into action. He stepped over Maddock's motionless figure and approached the window to gaze out at the approaches to the yard. Piercey was standing by the corral, gazing out beyond the yard, his eyes shaded by an upflung arm. Bannon peered in the same direction and spotted a puff of black gunsmoke drifting lazily on the breeze. He turned instantly and ran from the room, almost colliding with Sarah as she approached the door.

'The colonel has been shot,' Bannon said quickly, 'and I want to get the man who did it.'

He ran for the porch. At his back Sarah uttered a cry of shock and ran into the study.

5

Bannon dashed out of the house, swung into the saddle of his waiting horse and spurred the animal across the yard to bring it to a slithering halt in the dust beside Al Piercey, who was still gazing across the yard.

'The colonel has been shot,' Bannon rapped, 'and the bullet came from over there.'

'I thought I heard a shot. See that tall cactus on the other side of the creek? I figured a shot was fired from there. I ain't seen any movement so he might still be there.'

'You'd better get to the house and check on the colonel. I didn't get a chance to look at him. He could be dead.'

Bannon sent his horse around the corral, splashed into the creek and raced across to the cactus Piercey had indicated. His pistol was in his right hand, cocked and ready for action. He reined in beside the cactus and looked around. There were signs that the undergrowth had been flattened, and he caught the glint of an ejected rifle cartridge-case lying in the grass. He shifted his gaze to the middle distance, caught a movement higher up a slope, and spotted a rider disappearing over the crest. He saw only a head, which disappeared in the same instant, and sent the black forward at a gallop.

He was half-way up the slope when two riders came on to the crest and started shooting at him with pistols. Bannon gritted his teeth and ducked low over the black's neck. He triggered his Colt and sent three shots in rapid answer. One of the riders pitched sideways out of his saddle, the other turned instantly and departed. Bannon breathed shallowly through his mouth as gunsmoke flared around him, and the taste of black powder covered his lips.

Bannon swept over the crest and

reined in, his keen gaze taking in his surroundings. A horse was cropping grass only yards away, and a rider was galloping off into the undulations of the background. He turned his attention to the sprawled figure lying on the crest and holstered his gun, for the man was obviously dead — lying on his back with arms flung wide, and a large patch of blood on his chest.

Going closer, Bannon recognized Carter, who had taken Sarah earlier — one of Jex's men, he recalled. He fetched the man's horse and heaved the body across the saddle. The heavy silence of the range closed in around him as he remounted and cantered back to Sabre, leading the dead man's horse.

Several men were standing on the ranch house porch when Bannon reached it. They surrounded the dead man, dragged him from the horse, and stretched him out in the dust.

'Say, that's Rafe Carter,' someone declared.

'He rode for Mack Jex, didn't he?' Bannon demanded.

'Yeah! Him and a dozen other no-goods.'

'He's the man who grabbed the colonel's granddaughter, earlier,' Bannon said. 'How is the colonel?'

'We're waiting to hear. Billy Snell has gone to town to fetch Doc Keaton, so it ain't good.'

Bannon stepped over the porch and entered the house. He crossed the big living-room and made for the study. The door to the study was open. He peered in and saw Maddock lying on the floor with a cushion under his head, apparently unconscious. Sarah was bending over her grandfather, and a scowling Al Piercey was standing in the background. Maddock's shirt was open and there was blood showing on his chest.

'How is he?' Bannon enquired.

Sarah looked up at him, her face ashen in shock. Her hands were trembling.

'He's been shot through,' she declared. 'I've managed to stop the bleeding, and that's all I can do. Did you catch the man who shot him?'

Bannon nodded. 'There were two — and I had to kill one of them — Rafe Carter.'

'Jex's men.' Piercey straightened and made for the door. 'I'll take some of the boys into town and put Jex out of business. He's been causing trouble for years and it's about time someone shot the hell outa him.'

'I reckon you better stay here and do what you're paid to do,' Bannon retorted. 'You can't ride out at a time like this and leave the ranch unguarded.'

'He's right,' Sarah cut in. 'Would you leave the colonel and me defenceless, Al?'

'I'll ride into Clarkville and talk to Jex,' Bannon suggested. 'Better still, I'll bring him back here and you can talk to him.'

'You ain't gonna do a thing.' Piercey shook his head. 'This trouble flared up after you shot Hendry so you can fork your bronc and head out for other parts. With the colonel out of action, I'm running things around here, and you can get the hell out.'

'Where did you get that idea from?' Sarah demanded. 'I'll say what has to be done and who will do it. Pull in your horns, Al. You'll take orders from me or there will be real trouble around here. If you don't like it then you'd better ride out for other parts.'

Bannon could see that Piercey would not get his own way and prepared to depart.

'I'll head for town,' he said. 'I guess you won't budge from here while the colonel is on his back. Be seeing you.'

Sarah nodded and returned her attention to the colonel. Piercey glowered at Bannon but remained silent. Bannon went out to the porch and swung into his saddle. He rode out swiftly, his thoughts busy.

He had been sidetracked from his assignment by events at Sabre, and so far he had done nothing about locating the Parfitt gang. He needed to get his investigation moving, but felt he had to help sort out Sarah Maddock's problems before embarking on his own chores because he sensed it was all part of the general prevailing lawlessness. He rode steadily, wanting to reach Clarkville after dark, and the sun was barely below the western skyline when he caught his first glimpse of the lights of the town.

Mindful of the fact that Tom Arbuck's presence could complicate his plans, he dismounted outside the livery barn and led the black inside. The interior of the stable was gloomy, and Pete Lambert emerged from the office when he heard the sound of hoofs on the hard ground.

'So what happened after I rode out, Pete?' Bannon asked.

'You should have seen it,' the youth replied. 'I never knew Bixby had it in him. He told Arbuck to get out of town and not come back. I saw you ride in the direction of Sadilla so I told Arbuck you went south, and he headed out that way.'

'Thanks.' Bannon patted Lambert's shoulder. 'You did well, Pete. Now I want to see Mack Jex. Have you any idea where he might be at this time of the day?'

'If he ain't still in his office then he'll be at his house, I reckon. You want me to show you where he lives?'

'That would save me some time. Can you leave here?'

'Sure. There's not much doing at this time. Are you gonna give Jex hell?'

'It might pan out that way. You sound as if you'd like to see Jex get his come-uppance.'

'He's a bad man. It's about time someone put him on Boot Hill.'

'Is he mixed up with the bank-robbers operating around here?'

'I don't know about that.' Lambert sounded surprised by the thought. 'I know he runs some of the rustling that's going on, but they say that Hemp

Parfitt, the outlaw, has a gang that's hitting the banks out this way. Of course, Parfitt ain't above rustling when he gets the chance, and anything he steals in that line finds its way into Jex's hands.'

'Do you have any idea where the gang might be hiding out?' Bannon drew his gun and checked its loads, then spun the cylinder. He returned the weapon to its holster. 'I heard the sheriff has had no luck chasing Parfitt and his bunch.'

'Bixby couldn't catch a fly if it landed on his nose.' Disgust sounded in Lambert's voice.

'Did your father have any luck in that direction when he was the sheriff?' Bannon persisted.

'Well, no, he didn't, but that was because he could never raise a posse to help him hunt down Parfitt. He never even had a deputy; men were so scared of the outlaws.'

'OK. Just show me where Jex lives and I'll take it from there.' Bannon led the way out of the stable and they walked along the shadowy sidewalk into town.

Bannon was alert, and his right hand was close to the butt of his pistol as they traversed the wide street. The town was quiet, with few lights showing anywhere, except for the saloon, for most of the townsfolk had finished business for the day. Lambert paused at the door of Jex's office, which was in darkness. He tried the door, which was locked.

'Looks like he ain't here,' he said. 'I'll show you to his house. He's got a big place on East Street.'

They walked on. Bannon paused at the batwings of the saloon and peered inside, looking for Jex. There was no sign of the man and they continued.

'Is Jex married?' Bannon asked.

'No. He was seeing Bella Thompson for a spell but she left him some weeks ago and moved out of town. Right now he's living alone.'

They approached a side street where

several large houses were situated, and Lambert kept to the shadows as they continued. Lights showed in some of the buildings, but the house Lambert indicated as belonging to Jex was in darkness.

'He might be in the back of the house,' Lambert said.

They skirted the building only to find the rear in darkness.

'Have you any idea where he might be?' Bannon asked.

'There's no telling with Jex. He could be up to anything right now.'

'Well, thanks for showing me around. I won't keep you longer. I think I'll stick around here for a spell and wait for Jex to show up. Take care of my horse, will you? I'll settle up with you later.'

'OK.' Lambert grinned and departed.

Bannon heaved a sigh as he stepped into the shadow of a tree at the front of the house and prepared for a long wait, but barely ten minutes passed before a solitary figure appeared in the street and approached the house. He recognised Jex, drew his gun as Jex unlocked the front door, and stepped noiselessly behind the man as he entered the house. The muzzle of Bannon's pistol pressing against his spine halted Jex as if he had run into a wall. He froze and raised his hands. Bannon caught the smell of whiskey on Jex.

'What's this — robbery?' Jex demanded. 'Who are you?'

'Shut up and keep your hands clear of your body. I can see you well enough to plant a slug in your spine.'

Bannon used his left hand to take a match from a breast-pocket. He scraped it on the seat of his pants and held it up carefully when it flared. He saw a lamp standing on a small table in the entrance hall.

'Take the chimney off the lamp,' he ordered, and Jex obeyed.

Bannon touched the match to the wick of the lamp and yellow light filled the hall. Jex looked around at him as he replaced the chimney on the lamp, his eyes narrowing with sudden intention.

'What do you want?' he demanded. His right hand began to edge towards his left shoulder but he thought better of it and let the hand fall to his side.

'Why did two of your men grab Sarah Maddock on the trail near Sabre this morning?' Bannon demanded.

Jex shook his head. 'Are you joking? What would I want with her?'

'Rafe Carter works for you?'

'Sure. But I ain't seen him around all day.'

'And you won't see him again. I killed him after he'd shot Colonel Maddock out at Sabre.'

Jex's eyes narrowed to mere slits. 'Is Maddock dead?'

'We'll ride to Sabre and find out. If you're carrying a gun then get rid of it now.'

'Wait a minute. You take me out to Sabre and they'll kill me in cold blood.'

'I'm gonna do just that. You'll have to chance your future. You shouldn't mix in tough games if you can't take punishment. Come on. We'll get you a horse and ride out. On the way to Sabre you can tell me what the trouble is between you and Maddock, and why you had Sarah abducted. I don't like the thought of a girl being dragged into your dirty dealing.'

'I know nothing about her. What are you after? I can't leave here right now because I got business to attend to. Someone is calling on me shortly.'

'Your business can wait. I'm taking you to Sabre, so spare me an argument. Get your hands all the way up.'

Bannon relieved Jex of a snub-nosed pistol, shook him down for more weapons, and found a derringer in a vest-pocket. As he threw the weapons along the hall, Jex made a desperate play. He grabbed for Bannon's pistol and tried to wrest it from Bannon's hand. Bannon swung his left fist in a tight arc and planted his knuckles against Jex's jaw. Jex slumped, and Bannon caught hold of him by his shirt-front and eased him to the floor.

At that moment a boot scraped on hard ground outside the front door and Bannon whirled, his gun lifting. A tall man moved into the circle of light radiated by the lamp. He was dressed in dusty range clothes and was armed with a pistol in a cartridge-belt around his waist. His right hand dropped to the butt of his holstered gun when he saw the pistol in Bannon's hand, but then he stayed the movement and lifted his hand clear of his body.

'What's going on?' he demanded. 'Who's that on the floor?'

'Who are you and what's your business?' Bannon countered.

'I got business with Mack Jex,' the man replied easily. 'Is this his house? Are you Jex?'

'Yeah.' Bannon was quick-witted enough to take advantage of any chance that came his way. 'This guy tried to rob me. He was waiting in here in the dark when I came in.'

'Hemp sent me. He was expecting you at Owl Creek today.'

Bannon sharpened his gaze as he took in the man's features, and a thrill gripped him when he recognized Art Wiley, one of the Parfitt gang.

'I've got trouble around here,' he said sharply. 'Dave Hendry was shot, and a couple of my contacts from south of the border were killed.'

'You can't let anything come between you and Parfitt's business,' Wiley said unsympathetically. 'Have you got the girl yet?'

'My men had her this morning but some gunslick killed one of them and sprung her loose. Maddock has been shot, but I don't know yet if he's dead or not.'

'Sounds like you got things moving. Parfitt wants details of the bank in Sadilla. You were supposed to take care of that.'

'I haven't had a chance to go over that way yet. I hope to make the trip in the next few days, and I'll come out to Owl Creek soon as I can.'

'OK. I'll tell Parfitt what you say, but

he ain't gonna like being held up like this. You better get moving, but fast. We'll be at Owl Creek for a couple more days, but after that we'll be on the move again, back to the hide-out in Pronghorn Valley.

Bannon nodded as Wiley turned to depart. He was undecided about letting the outlaw go, and almost called the man back but stopped himself. Wiley slipped away like a shadow. Bannon bent over Jex, who was beginning to stir, and dragged him to his feet.

'You're going to jail but fast,' Bannon said grimly. 'Whatever your business, you're out of it now. Get moving, and don't give me any trouble.'

Jex remained silent as they walked to the main street and headed for the jail. Bannon kept the muzzle of his pistol jammed against Jex's side until they reached the door of the law office. Jex opened the door and stepped into the office, his hands raised shoulder high.

Ed Bixby, alone in the office, was seated behind his desk. His hat was off and his sleeves were rolled up. He looked up quickly at their entrance.

'What's this?' he demanded.

'Put Jex behind bars and I'll tell you,' Bannon replied. 'It's time you got down to your duty, Sheriff. You don't know it yet, but we are going to work together.'

'Tom Arbuck said you're Kell Bannon, the outlaw,' Bixby declared. 'He's after you for the price on your head, so what are you up to, coming in here with a gun on Jex?'

'Lock him up and then I'll tell you,' Bannon insisted.

'On what charge? I can't just throw a man in the cells.'

Bannon suppressed a sigh. 'Rafe Carter abducted Sarah Maddock this morning.' He went on to explain the events that had taken place, and when he spoke of the colonel getting shot, and the subsequent action in which Carter was killed, Bixby picked up a bunch of keys off a corner of his desk.

'I don't know what the hell is going on, what with you being a wanted outlaw and all, but if what you're saying is true then I'll throw Jex in the jail and lose the key. I've been keen to jug him for a long time.'

'You can't take the word of an outlaw against me,' Jex protested.

'I'm a special deputy marshal working under cover,' Bannon said quietly. He produced a piece of black satin cloth from a breast pocket and unfolded it to reveal a glinting law badge — a small star embossed on a silver shield. 'You can contact Governor Mayhew's office, Sheriff. I'm here to set up the Parfitt gang, and I shall need your help. Now let's get down to business and start by putting Jex behind bars.'

Jex was still protesting when a cell door clanged shut on him and Bixby turned the key. The sheriff led the way back into his office and sat down at his desk, grinning uneasily, his eyes narrowed and glinting. Bannon stood before him, tall and forbidding, his face expressionless.

'Do you expect me to believe you're a deputy marshal?' Bixby demanded.

'You don't have to take my word for it. I've got papers in my saddle-bags, but in any case, I expect you to check on me with my office. Until then you can give me the benefit of the doubt. I've heard some strange stories about you, Sheriff, and you better understand from the outset that I expect you to do your duty to the best of your ability, because if you don't you'll be sharing that cell with Jex so fast your feet won't touch the ground.'

'You ain't got no cause to threaten me. I've always done my best in this county, but the dice have been stacked against me from the start. If you are who you say then I'll back you to the hilt. I can't say fairer than that.'

'Send a wire to the governor's office. Keep Jex in jail until I get back. I'm going out to Sabre to check on the situation there.'

'You'd better watch out for Arbuck. He's plumb loco when it comes to collecting bounty.'

'I'll handle Arbuck if I have to,' Bannon replied. 'See you later, Sheriff. Keep what I've told you under your hat. I'm supposed to be working under cover.' He paused before asking: 'Where is Owl Creek?'

'Heck. That is where I first set eyes on you. Jake Garner's place is on Owl Creek.'

'Thanks.' Bannon departed, his thoughts already busy on what he had to do. Art Wiley had said Parfitt and his bunch were at Owl Creek. Did that mean Bella Thompson was in trouble?

He hurried back to the stable, wishing he could be in two places at once, but by the time he had the black ready for travel he had decided to visit Owl Creek. His first duty was to the assignment Governor Mayhew had given him. If Hemp Parfitt was at Owl Creek then the sooner he checked out the place the better.

Starshine gave him sufficient light to make his way across the shadowed range. He rode steadily, reaching Owl Creek in the grey light of dawn. A faint suspicion of crimson was already showing along the eastern horizon, and he dismounted across the creek from the ranch and eased forward through a stand of cottonwoods to look over the spread. Lights were showing at several windows, and he figured it was too early for Bella to be up and about unless she had visitors.

The corral at the rear of the cabin contained eleven horses, and it did not take Bannon long to spot an armed guard, concealed where he could watch the approaches to the spread.

A tingle of excitement made its presence felt in Bannon's chest. He circled the creek and hunkered down in bushes close to the well, wanting to discover why a gang of notorious bank robbers was here. As daylight approached the guard came out of his position and made a round of the yard before going into the house. Bannon could hear his voice as he roused the men inside. Smoke began to rise from the chimney. A few minutes later Bella appeared in the doorway of the house, carrying a bucket, and made her way to the well.

Bannon could tell by the expression on Bella's face that she was not pleased with the presence of her visitors.

'Bella,' he called. 'Carry on with what you're doing. I'm Bannon. What's going on here?'

Bella's expression changed but she did not falter in her actions. She lowered a bucket on a rope into the well and Bannon heard it splash on the surface of the water.

'Hemp Parfitt turned up here yesterday with some of his bunch,' she said quietly. 'From what he's said, I think he's waiting for a contact to come here.'

'Mack Jex,' Bannon informed her. 'But Jex is in jail. Are you being held prisoner?'

'Parfitt has made it clear that I can't leave. He still thinks everything is OK between Jex and me, which puts me on his side. What are you going to do? You can't fight the whole bunch of them.'

'And I can't let them ride away from here,' Bannon responded grimly.

Bella pulled up a brimming bucket of water from the well and poured it into the bucket she had brought.

'If I were you I'd go back to town, round up a posse, and then come back. You might catch Parfitt flat-footed. I think he plans to stick around here for another day at least. I've got to go now. I'm being watched closely.'

Bannon saw the guard emerge from the house and come towards the well. Bella turned abruptly and began to lug the bucket of water back to the house. Bannon hunched lower in concealment, pistol in his hand. He watched Bella set down the bucket when the guard reached her.

'You could carry this into the house for me,' she said.

The guard kicked over the bucket with a dusty toe. He dropped his rifle, drew a pistol, and grabbed Bella, swinging her around until she was between him and Bannon's position.

'Who's that hiding in the bushes by the well?' he demanded. 'I spotted him.' He raised his voice. 'Hey, you in the bushes, come on out with your hands up. I got you dead to rights. Don't try anything or Bella will get a slug in the head.'

Bannon froze for an interminable moment. He saw the guard put the muzzle of the pistol to Bella's head. He holstered his own gun and stood up immediately, lifting his hands clear of his body as he did so. His brain was needle-sharp as he went forward. He was ready to bluff his way out of the grim situation that encompassed him.

6

'Who are you?' the guard demanded, 'and why are you sneaking around here?'

'I dropped by to see Bella,' Bannon replied, 'and when I saw all the horses here I decided to play it careful. I'm Kelly. I work for Mack Jex. He asked me to stop by to check that Bella is OK.'

The guard relaxed visibly at the mention of Jex's name, and Bannon saw Bella narrow her eyes at his fabrication, but the outlaw kept him covered with his pistol.

'You better talk to Hemp,' he said. 'He's in the house. I'll help Bella get another bucket of water.'

Bannon walked to the house. An outlaw appeared in the doorway and watched his approach. Cal Garner appeared beside the outlaw, his boyish face showing dislike of the bad men.

'How-do, Cal?' Bannon greeted. The boy turned and went back into the house without replying.

'What's your business?' the outlaw demanded.

Bannon smiled as the man's name came to mind: Frank Pardoe, one of the more prominent outlaws of Hemp Parfitt's gang.

'I'll tell that to Parfitt,' Bannon replied.

A tall, broad-shouldered man, whose fleshy face was heavily bearded, stepped into the doorway. He dropped his hands to the twin butts of Colt Peacemakers holstered at his waist. His narrowed brown eyes were hard, filled with suspicion, and he regarded Bannon for a moment. Hemp Parfitt in the flesh, Bannon thought, the fingers of his gun hand tingling. If he could take these outlaws now his job would be at an end, but he dismissed the thought instantly. This was not the time or the place.

'Who in hell are you?' Parfitt demanded at length.

'The name is Kelly. I work for Mack Jex. Your man Art Wiley saw Jex last night and talked about the bank in Sadilla. I'm on my way there now to get the information you want, and Jex asked me to drop by here to check on Bella.'

'I told Jex to keep this quiet.' Parfitt scowled. 'Does the whole county know I'm planning to hit the bank in Sadilla?'

'You don't think Jex does all the running about for you personally, do you?' Bannon countered.

'I don't like this.' Parfitt shook his head. 'Pardoe, tell the boys to saddle up. We're riding out pronto.'

'Let's have breakfast first,' Pardoe protested.

'No time for that. We'll split the breeze. I don't like this set-up. Anyone could ride in here claiming to be working for us. I told Jex to play it safe. Where is Wiley, anyway — why didn't he come straight back from Clarkville like I told him?'

'Mebbe he visited a saloon.' Pardoe scowled.

Parfitt returned his attention to Bannon. 'You better get outa here and do what you set out to do,' he said. 'Tell Jex I'll be at the big hide-out for a couple of weeks, and he better start jumping around to do like I asked him.'

'Sure.' Bannon nodded. 'I'll have breakfast before I ride out.'

Parfitt turned on his heel and bellowed orders. Outlaws appeared and hurried out to the corral. Bella returned with the guard. Her face was taut as she watched the gang's hurried departure. Bannon heaved a sigh of relief when Parfitt rode out at the head of his men. Bella wilted visibly when they were alone.

'I didn't think you would survive when you were spotted,' she said. 'What did you tell Parfitt that had him and his bunch jumping on their horses and riding out?'

'I got lucky, I guess. Parfitt said he was heading for the big hide-out. Have you got any idea where that is?'

Bella smiled. 'If I had learned that I

would have informed Governor Mayhew.'

'Then I'd better get on their trail and find it for myself,' Bannon mused. 'If breakfast is ready I'll eat before I hit the trail.'

'But you can't follow the gang just like that!' Bella shook her head. 'Parfitt is full of tricks.'

'Don't worry about that.' Bannon smiled. 'This is a big chance to get Parfitt and his boys. If we can catch him in his hideout he'll be finished. Now hurry up with that breakfast. I've got a big day to look forward to.'

Bannon knew there was no hurry to hit the trail after the gang. He was expert at following sign, and if the outlaws left any kind of a trail he would follow it clear into hell. He took care of his horse while Bella put the finishing touches to breakfast and, after eating, he set out after the gang.

The tracks he followed were plain upon the dusty ground and he trailed northward a couple of miles behind Parfitt and his bunch. But he had barely travelled a mile when he found the tracks of three horses cutting in from the right and joining those left by the outlaws. He reined in and looked around, his mind working fast. Were these newcomers some more of the gang? He went on warily, watching for movement ahead, until he caught sight of a trio of riders apparently trailing the gang. He dropped back several yards and followed.

Bannon reined in just below the crest of a ridge, dismounted and reached into his saddle-bag for his field glasses. He focused on the three riders, and his teeth clicked together when the bearlike figure of Tom Arbuck appeared. Arbuck! Bannon shook his head. That complicated matters. Arbuck was not going to quit until he had got what he was after, and that was Kell Bannon. Governor Mayhew's scheme to use an outlaw's notoriety against a gang of bank-robbers looked like coming unstuck.

Bannon followed Arbuck at a safe distance. The bounty hunter was evidently tracking the Parfitt gang, and it was in Bannon's mind to try and get Arbuck to help him nail the outlaws, but he knew Arbuck had a one-track mind, and if the bounty hunter had set out to catch Kell Bannon then nothing would divert him. True, he might go for the bigger rewards available on the Parfitt bunch, but eventually Arbuck would make a play for his original target.

But why was Arbuck trailing the gang? Did he fancy his chance against a dozen hard-bitten outlaws? Bannon dropped back to a safe distance and followed, using great stealth and guile. Twice he saw one of the men with Arbuck rein about and study their back trail, checking to see if they in turn were being followed. Parfitt and his bunch were pushing on as if they had no cares in the world.

Long, hot hours passed monotonously and the terrain began to change in character, grassy plain giving way to hills and arroyos. The sun was way over to the west. Bannon moved even more warily, and was startled when a burst of gunfire ahead hammered out in the silence and echoes grumbled away to the horizon. He rode to the nearest crest to observe. His eyes glinted when he saw a figure sprawled on the ground ahead and Arbuck and another of his sidekicks heading for deep cover.

Parfitt and his gang were appearing on a crest further ahead, and three of the outlaws set out in pursuit of the surviving bounty hunters. Bannon watched intently. When pursued and pursuers disappeared from sight the rest of the gang turned and rode on. Bannon remained motionless, considering the situation, aware that he could not continue tracking the bunch until all the members of the gang were together again. Minutes later he heard shooting coming from the direction Arbuck had taken, and the sound galvanized him into action. His patience was strained as he spurred his horse forward and set out in the direction of the disturbance.

The bounty hunter had entered a gully with his remaining sidekick, and three outlaws were following them. Gun echoes were still grumbling away into the distance. Bannon eased his pistol from its holster and carried it in his right hand as he pushed on. The gully led up into rising ground, narrowing considerably as it ascended, and suddenly there was a horse blocking the way, its rider crumpled in the dust. Bannon dismounted and went forward to check.

He found the outlaw Frank Pardoe dead with a bullet hole in the centre of his chest. Bannon shook his head, aware that Tom Arbuck was a man who should never be underestimated. He led his horse past the spot and remounted, his keen gaze fixed on the upper reaches of the gully, his nerve taut and his gun ready for action.

The upper end of the gully petered out in a rocky place where the ground undulated and rose steeply to low hills in the background. Tracks led away west, and Bannon reined in. He used his field glasses to check his surroundings, and caught sight of movement a long way above his position. Two riders were galloping over a ridge where streamers of dust marked the passage of Arbuck and his remaining sidekick.

Bannon followed, aware that he was being led away from his main objective. But two of the outlaw gang were ahead, and the tracks of the rest of the gang were plain on the ground back where he had left them. He had no desire to place himself between two factions of the gang, and if he could eliminate the outlaws ahead the overall odds would be easier to face. He pushed forward resolutely, aware that the men ahead — outlaws and bounty hunters — would not desist until one side or the other was out of it.

More shooting from ahead warned Bannon that Arbuck had finally turned to fight. He closed in cautiously until he could see a cluster of rocks where gun smoke was drifting thickly. There were two gun positions in front of the rocks where the outlaws were down in cover and engaging the bounty hunters.

Bannon dismounted in cover, trailed his reins and took his rifle along as he crawled forward to close in on the action. Twice he heard flying lead pass closely over him, but the shots had not been aimed directly at him. He reached the spot where the outlaws had left their horses. He circled it, intent on getting into the fight, and edged in behind the nearest of the outlaws.

He was only feet behind his target when the man rose up to fire his rifle and Arbuck shot him. The outlaw groaned and relaxed, and the second outlaw began to withdraw. He fired three quick shots at the rocks and then slithered back to where his horse was waiting. Arbuck and his sidekick intensified their shooting, and more lead crackled around Bannon, who rolled into a depression and kept his head down.

The outlaw rolled into Bannon's cover, gasping for breath. Bannon thrust the muzzle of his pistol against the man's chest, his left hand knocking aside the man's rifle.

'Stay quiet,' Bannon told him.

Arbuck and his sidekick stopped shooting and an uneasy silence settled over the rocks. Moments later the sound of receding hoofs reached Bannon's ears. He disarmed his prisoner, and by the time he was able to take a look in Arbuck's direction all he saw was the bounty hunter disappearing fast into the distance. He turned his attention back to his prisoner.

'Rube Otter,' he said, recognizing the outlaw, who frowned and glared at him with surprise dawning in his expression.

'Say, you're the guy who rode into Owl Creek this morning with a message for Parfitt.' Otter was middle-aged and gaunt-faced. 'Weren't you on your way to Sadilla?'

'I'm taking the long way,' Bannon

replied. 'Do you know who you were shooting at?'

'Yeah; that damn bounty hunter, Tom Arbuck, somehow got on our trail. Parfitt sent three of us to nail him.'

'And you failed. Arbuck is a tough nut to crack. I crossed his trail just after leaving Owl Creek, and when I saw he was trailing Parfitt I tagged along to see what would happen. You took out after him before I could warn the gang.'

'So what happens now?'

'You go back to Parfitt and I'll ride to Sadilla.' Bannon grinned.

'How come you didn't take a hand in shooting at Arbuck? Between us, we might have got him.'

'He was on my trail before he picked up the tracks of the gang,' Bannon replied. 'He almost got me in Clarkville, and I don't wanta tangle with him. Your bunch should be able to take care of him.'

Bannon went back to where he had left his horse. He watched Otter check his sidekick before moving off, and waited patiently to fall in behind and follow at a distance. The sun was close to the western horizon now, and he wondered how far it was to the big hideout. He stayed well behind Otter, and full darkness came while he was ascending a long rise.

He made camp, ate a frugal meal, and turned in to sleep peacefully until the first rays of the rising sun touched his face. When he hit the trail again he found the tracks easy to follow, but was aware that he had run out of excuses for trailing the gang if he should happen to be seen. He watched for signs of Arbuck, although he knew the bounty hunter would never betray himself through carelessness.

The black needed a rest when they reached a water hole, and Bannon saw signs of the gang's passing while he sat in the shade of a rock and gave the horse a breather. He was about to go on when he heard the sound of hoofs close by and peered around a rock to see Al Piercey riding steadily in the direction taken by the gang.

The Sabre ramrod did not appear to be watching tracks but rode as if he knew where he was going. He looked neither to left nor right and did not turn off to the water hole. Bannon sat frowning while he considered. What was Piercey doing out here; riding like a man on a one-way trail?

He moved out behind the ramrod and followed. Piercey seemed to have no interest in his surroundings, and did not look around at all while he continued at a canter. Noon passed and the afternoon wore on. The terrain was rocky and desolate, and a heavy silence lay over it like a blanket. They were heading for a great buttress of bare rock that rose up in steep escarpments and barred all further progress. Piercey angled to the right, entered a narrow defile, and disappeared from view.

Bannon rode into deep cover outside the defile and dismounted. He took care of his horse and allowed it to drink water from his hat before taking his rifle and leaving the animal. Shadows were closing in as he made his way on foot to the narrow defile and entered. There was barely room for a rider to pass through. He saw signs that a number of horses had entered recently, and went forward slowly.

The defile ended after Bannon had counted 120 paces. He crouched just inside the exit and peered into a wide, rolling valley — an expanse of lush grass that was hemmed in by tall rock walls. He was surprised to see a small herd of cattle in the distance, and there was a glitter of water over to the left, showing through a screen of cotton-woods, about 200 yards from the entrance. Bannon caught the indistinct shape of a shack half-hidden by the trees, and beyond that was an empty corral.

He saw Piercey ride into the shade of the cottonwoods, so he set out through long grass to approach the trees. The sight of the empty corral bothered him, for Hemp Parfitt and the gang had ridden in here only hours before. A breeze rustled through the long grass. The sky was darkening. Nightfall was barely an hour away. He reached the fringe of cottonwoods and paused within their cover, straining his eyes to search his dangerous surroundings. Piercey's horse was standing hipshot by the door of the shack, and at that moment a shot boomed close by, sending a string of hollow echoes across the valley.

Bannon sneaked forward until he could see the shack clearly. The door was open, and Piercey was in the act of dragging a body outside. The Sabre ramrod paused when the body was clear of the shack and glanced around before re-entering the ramshackle little building. Bannon listened to the sounds of furniture being moved around, and began to circle the shack. He reached the stream that meandered nearby and crossed it to ease in against the left-hand wall of the shack. A crack in the sun-warped boards enabled him to peer inside.

He saw Piercey in the dim interior, crouching by the stone fireplace at the back of the building. Three large flat stones had been removed from the fire-blackened hearth and Piercey was in the act of opening two saddle-bags which he had removed from the cavity beneath. Bannon narrowed his eyes when he saw the contents of the bags: wads of greenbacks, the proceeds of bank-raids the Parfitt gang had made, he surmised.

So where was the gang? The thought lay uppermost in Bannon's mind as he watched Piercey. Had Parfitt been scared off by the activity on his back trail? Bannon mentally cursed Arbuck for showing up. The bounty hunter was adding to the problems he was facing.

As Piercey moved to leave the shack, Bannon eased round to the nearest front corner, drawing his pistol as he did so, keeping his Winchester in his left hand. When Piercey emerged into the open Bannon stepped forward, gun levelled. Piercey caught the movement and froze instantly, his eyes narrowing.

'Caught you with your hand in the honey-pot,' Bannon observed. 'What gives, Piercey?'

'What in hell are you doing here?' Piercey had the two bulging saddle-bags across his left shoulder. His right hand was down at his side.

'I was about to ask you that.' Bannon smiled. 'What are you doing in Parfitt's hideout; stealing his loot?'

'Someone has got to put a crimp in Parfitt's tail He's got too big for his boots. It was one of Jex's men shot Colonel Maddock, but Parfitt gave the orders. I reckoned the best way to get Parfitt to pull out was to come in here and steal his dough.'

'What's your connection with Parfitt?'

'I don't have a connection. I work for the colonel, and do like he tells me. He's the man who pays my wages.'

'Is Maddock in with Parfitt?' Bannon turned the thought over in his mind. 'If they are partners then why would

Parfitt want Jex to abduct Sarah Maddock?'

'Don't ask me, ask the colonel. Like I said, he's running the business. I just do what I'm told.' Piercey grinned crookedly. 'I'm right about you, huh? You ain't no ordinary line rider. You're a lawman, ain't you? I got the smell of you the minute you walked into that saloon in Clarkville. A lot of men figured they could walk into this county and clean up on the gangs, and most of them are buried. I told the colonel about you but he wouldn't listen. So you reckon to come out on top of the pile, huh? Well, you won't do that unless I help you, and my fee for turning against the colonel will be what I'm holding in these two saddle-bags.'

'That's stolen money and will have to go back to the rightful owners,' Bannon said. 'I don't need your help, Piercey. I'm gonna take you to Clarkville and jail you. It's obvious that Parfitt and his gang have kept moving, and they ain't likely to come back here in a hurry.

They will come back eventually to collect that dough, and you just killed the man they left to watch it. When they do show up I'll have a bunch of lawmen waiting for them. So forget about keeping that dough. Put down the bags and get your hands up. You're out of this now.'

Piercey grimaced and shifted the saddle-bags from his shoulder. He made as if to throw them on the ground in front of Bannon, but flicked his powerful wrist and hurled them into Bannon's face, lunging forward as Bannon ducked and sidestepped.

The heavy bags caught Bannon's right shoulder and knocked him off balance. His gun-hand dropped away although he retained his grasp on the Colt. The next instant Piercey collided with him, his powerful arms wrapping around Bannon in a bear hug that trapped Bannon's arms to his sides. Bannon allowed himself to fall to the ground, taking Piercey with him, and head-butted Piercey on the way down, catching the man's nose with his forehead. Piercey cursed and released his hold. He scrambled to his feet, at the same time reaching for his holstered gun. Bannon thrust a foot between Piercey's legs and sent him crashing to the ground.

Bannon got to his feet and levelled his pistol. Piercey was rolling, and came up on his elbows, pistol lifting in Bannon's direction despite the fact that Bannon held the advantage. Bannon thumbed off a shot and dust flew from Piercey's right shoulder. He uttered a cry and dropped his gun. Blood spurted from his chest and soaked into his shirt. He stared at Bannon for an interminable moment before falling back senseless.

Bannon listened to the receding echoes of the shot, his eyes on Piercey. He holstered his pistol, and was about to go forward to check Piercey when a shadow from behind moved into his field of vision. He whirled, his right hand flashing to the butt of his gun, and then he stopped the movement, for Tom Arbuck was standing a few feet behind him, a gun levelled in his great paw of a hand and a wide grin on his bearded face.

7

A red-lipped gap appeared in Arbuck's straggly beard where his mouth was situated and a chuckle rumbled from deep within him. He waggled the pistol in his hand, and kept his eyes on Bannon as he gave a signal with his left hand. Moments later a rider appeared, leading Arbuck's horse, and came up at a canter.

'You got him, Tom,' the newcomer observed, springing out of his saddle and hurrying around Bannon to relieve him of his pistol. He kicked aside the Winchester Bannon had dropped and then produced a set of cuffs and snapped them around Bannon's wrists. 'Who's this other guy?'

'I ain't got around to asking him yet.' Arbuck's voice sounded like gravel hitting a tin roof. 'Take a look in the shack and make sure we're alone, Bill.

Looks like they killed the man left behind to look after Parfitt's loot.' He gazed at Bannon for a moment. 'That is what's in those two saddle-bags, huh?'

Bannon nodded. 'Listen, Arbuck, we can do a deal. You'd rather pick up the whole of the Parfitt gang than take me in, wouldn't you?'

'I've been trailing you for weeks, Bannon, and you're worth two thousand dollars to me. If I go for the Parfitt gang I'll likely get myself killed. So who are these guys you got here? Did you and your pards fall out over Parfitt's loot?'

Bannon pointed to Piercey. 'He's Colonel Maddock's ramrod at Sabre — Al Piercey. He got tired of riding for Maddock and decided to pick up Parfitt's cache. I came in behind him, looking for Parfitt, and caught him in the act. He shot that guy over there as I arrived, and I haven't had a chance to see who it is he nailed. It's one of the gang, sure enough, left to guard the money, and there'll be a price on his head.'

'Check the irons on Bannon and look over that other guy,' Arbuck told his sidekick. He grinned. 'This could be my lucky day. We saw the gang ride out of the top pass and came in here to look for the dough. There's a reward for its return, and that'll be rich pickings.'

'You'll be making a big mistake if you don't listen to me,' Bannon observed. 'Take a look in my left-hand breast-pocket. I'm not an outlaw. I'm a state deputy marshal. My job is to work under cover and set up Parfitt's gang for a clean-up. Take me in and you'll learn the truth, but I don't want to lose Parfitt's trail now I've got this close to him.'

'Search him, Bill, and watch out for tricks. They say he's smarter than a wagonload of monkeys.'

Bannon was searched by the grinning sidekick, and Arbuck grimaced when he saw the law badge Bannon carried.

'So you killed some poor dope of a lawman and stole his badge, huh?' Arbuck shook his head. 'No dice,

Bannon. I got you dead to rights and you're gonna pay the price for your wrongdoing.'

'You've got a one-track mind,' Bannon insisted. 'You've been riding the back trails and tracking outlaws too long. Look at that sheaf of papers you've got in your hand. They're the latest wanted dodgers on the prominent members of Parfitt's gang. I tell you I'm a deputy marshal after the gang, and you could make a rich haul throwing in with me to take them. I can't collect on any of the outlaws I arrest, but if you're with me you can claim all the bounty available.'

'Sounds like a good bet, Tom,' Bill said. 'What have we got to lose? We're two to one, and if we don't let him have his gun back there ain't much he can do.'

'I don't trust him.' Arbuck shook his head. 'We've put in a lot of time and trouble to corner him. We'll take him back to Clarkville and talk to Sheriff Bixby. That old coot will put us straight.'

Bannon sighed and resigned himself to the situation. He knew Arbuck was single-minded, and no amount of talking would dissuade him from his course of action. He watched Arbuck cross to the man Piercey had killed and saw him check his face against the pictures on the wanted posters. Arbuck grinned and came back to Bannon.

'That's Jed Spokane lying there,' he announced. 'He's worth a cool three thousand bucks. That ain't chicken-feed! Is there a price on Piercey's head?'

'Not that I know of!' Bannon shook his head. 'Is Piercey alive?'

'Check him out, Bill,' Arbuck directed. 'We'll leave him if he's dead. He ain't worth anything to us.'

Bill approached Piercey and bent to examine him. 'He's still breathing,' he said, 'but he don't look like he'll last long. If we take him with us he'll be dead before we reach Clarkville.'

'Leave him then. Get Spokane's body across a saddle and we'll pull out.

Bannon, don't give me any trouble on the ride to town or I'll plug you and tote you in dead.'

'You'll kick yourself when you learn the truth, Arbuck,' Bannon replied. 'You've got the chance of picking up a fortune on the Parfitt gang but you'll end up with nothing if you take me back to Clarkville.'

'Climb into your saddle and we'll hit the trail,' Arbuck rasped.

Bannon had no option but to obey. They rode back through the wilderness in the direction of Clarkville, arriving within sight of the town during the middle of the afternoon of the third day. Bannon had chafed inwardly during the long ride. Arbuck had remained mostly silent on the trail while his sidekick had scouted backwards and forwards around them, watching for signs of the outlaws.

Sheriff Bixby was seated at his desk when they entered the law office, his eyes closed and his head resting in his cupped hands. He looked up when

Arbuck slammed the street door, and sprang to his feet when he recognized his visitors.

'What's goin' on?' he demanded.

'I got me some bad men,' Arbuck replied. 'One dead outlaw across his saddle, name of Spokane, and this one is Kell Bannon, worth two thousand dollars.'

'This one is a state deputy marshal,' Bixby retorted. 'He's working under cover. Looks like you've come unstuck this time, Arbuck.'

'So you fell for that line, huh?' Arbuck grinned. 'He tried to fool me with that story.'

'Don't take my word for it.' Bixby picked up a paper from his desk and held it out. 'Read it for yourself. This is from the governor's office in Austin. I got it two days ago.'

Arbuck took the paper and scanned it, his eyes narrowing as he grasped the import of what was written. Bannon held out his arms.

'You can take these cuffs off now,

Arbuck,' he said. 'We could have made quite a killing in Pronghorn Valley if you'd listened to me.'

Arbuck shook his head, finding it difficult to accept that the price on Bannon's head was bogus.

'I've been looking at your dodgers for years,' he said slowly. 'Who in hell thought up that sneaky way of getting at the outlaws? I've wasted a lot of time and effort tracking you down, and it's cost me a pile of dough.'

'You'll get the bounty on Spokane, and the reward they're offering for the recovery of the dough you've got in those saddle-bags,' Bannon rasped, 'so take these cuffs off me and I'll get on with what I'm supposed to do.'

Arbuck glanced at the paper again, even yet reluctant to accept the situation. Then he heaved a sigh, produced the key to the handcuffs, and set Bannon free. He explained to Bixby what had occurred in Pronghorn Valley and dumped the bulging saddle-bags on the desk.

'Count that and we'll agree the figure,' he said. 'I want the dough for recovering it pronto.'

'What's been happening around here while I've been gone?' Bannon cut in. 'Have you heard from Sabre? Is Colonel Maddock alive? Is Jex still behind bars?'

'I sent a deputy out to Sabre to check. Maddock is here in town now, at Doc Keaton's place. They reckon he'll live. Jex is still behind bars. I need a report from you stating what he's to be charged with, or I'll have to release him.'

'He's guilty of rustling, and supplying the Parfitt gang with information about the banks that are being robbed. There's a herd of cattle in Pronghorn Valley that needs to be checked out and returned to their rightful owners. Right now I need to ride out to Owl Creek. I'll get back here soon as I can.' Bannon looked at Arbuck. 'Stay out of my way,' he warned. 'Why don't you go back to Pronghorn Valley and set an ambush for

Parfitt? When I get some help in here there won't be any pickings for the likes of you.'

Bannon left the office. Clarkville was quiet, with hardly anyone on the street. Five horses were standing hipshot at a hitching-rail in front of a saloon. He took up his reins and led his black along the street to the stable, needing a fresh horse to continue. He was passing the hotel when a woman called him and he turned to see Sarah Maddock emerging from the building, her soft features harshly set.

'Miss Sarah,' he acknowledged, touching the brim of his Stetson with a long forefinger. 'How is the colonel doing? I was about to get a fresh horse from the barn and ride out to Sabre to see you. Maybe you can help me with a problem that's come up.'

'The colonel is making progress,' she replied. 'Doc says he will recover but it will be slow. I've been up to my neck in problems, trying to run the ranch. Al Piercey has quit cold and I can't find a good foreman to take his place.'

'Tell me about Piercey,' Bannon said. 'Why did he quit?'

'He wouldn't let me run the ranch after Grandfather was shot. There was a bad argument, and he quit cold. I was shocked. He had been with Grandfather in the army. I wish he would come back. There's so much to do, and I don't like to leave town while Grandfather is helpless.'

Bannon told her about the incidents that had occurred in Pronghorn Valley, and saw horror dawn in her expression when he mentioned Al Piercey. She shook her head in disbelief.

'Al would never do anything to hurt Grandfather!' she gasped.

'He rode into Parfitt's hideout as if he knew exactly where he was going, shot an outlaw, and was taking a cache of stolen bank money when I got the drop on him. There's no doubt in my mind that he was stealing that money. I had to shoot him, and he was dying when I started back for town. I should think he's dead by now.'

'He never did anything to suggest he might be crooked,' Sarah said. 'He was hard-working. Of course he had that strange thing about bracing and bullying every man who showed up at the ranch looking for work, but he lived and breathed Sabre.'

'We'll get to the bottom of it before it's over,' Bannon mused. 'Are you staying in town now?'

'I don't like to be too far away from Grandfather while he's helpless. Sheriff Bixby told me you had put Jex in jail so I had nothing to worry about from him. Jex's office is closed and none of his men are around except Dave Hendry, who is still not on his feet, but recovering from his wound.'

'Jex is finished around here.' Bannon nodded, his keen gaze searching the street. 'I've got the deadwood on him. He'll be behind bars for a very long time.'

'You're a lawman, aren't you?' Sarah asked.

Bannon smiled. 'Let's change the subject. I have to get moving. I'll be back in town later and then I'll talk to you some more.'

Sarah nodded and turned away. Bannon glanced around the street and his gaze sharpened when he saw two men emerging from an alley almost opposite the law office. Both were wearing sombreros, and one had a pistol in his right hand. Bannon reached for his gun and drew it smoothly. Two more Mexicans appeared on the street from the alley beside the jail and the two across the street left the alley opposite to join them. Bannon started to hurry forward as they converged on the jail.

He was still thirty yards from the law office when the first of the Mexicans thrust open the door and disappeared inside, followed by two of the others. The fourth Mexican paused at the doorway and turned to look around the street. He saw Bannon approaching, gun in hand, and reached for his holstered pistol.

Bannon triggered a shot that struck the Mexican in the chest. The man twisted and fell heavily. Bannon did not break his stride. He went forward, gun ready, and reached the door of the law office just as a Mexican stuck his head out to check on the shot that had been fired. Bannon fired again, his shot taking the man in the throat, and he lunged forward into the office, leaping over the falling body.

Two shots were fired at him and he went down on his knees, gun blasting. Bixby was seated at his desk, hands shoulder high, his craggy face a taut mask. The two Mexicans were crouching and facing the door as Bannon burst in on them. Gunsmoke was flaring across the small room and Bannon added to it with a burst of rapid shooting. The office shook to the quick gun blasts, and both Mexicans went sprawling lifelessly. Bannon reloaded his smoking pistol, his eyes steady on the shocked sheriff.

Bixby pushed himself to his feet and

came unsteadily around the desk.

'They walked in on me and got me cold,' he said thickly. 'They came for Jex. Hendry was in here with another Mexican, and they took Jex out the back door, where horses were waiting.'

'Where are your two deputies?' Bannon demanded. 'There should be more than one man on duty when you've got prisoners in the cells.'

'The law is stretched mighty thin in these parts,' Bixby retorted.

'So Hendry came in first and took Jex.' Bannon's keen eyes bored into Bixby, who seemed to quail. 'What did these four want after Hendry pulled out?'

'I guess they were gonna finish me off.' Bixby shook his head. His face was pale under its tan and his hands were trembling.

'You'd better sit down at the desk before you fall down,' Bannon suggested. 'And fill me in on what's been going on around here. You haven't dealt the law as it should have been handled.

There are reports about you in the governor's office that hint you are working with Parfitt and his gang.'

'That's not true! I've done everything I can to run the law right, but I never got the support I needed.'

'Well I'm here now and things are gonna be a lot different from here on in. Get a posse together and ride out to Pronghorn Valley. Al Piercey will be dead, so look for Parfitt's tracks and get on his trail. Find out where's he's gone — he rode into the valley but kept going, and he could return there at any time. I've got one or two loose ends around here to sort through, but later I'll be on my way back to Parfitt's hideout, and I want to find you busy tracking the gang.'

Bixby nodded. Bannon walked through the cells to the back door. He found the prints of three horses in the dust of the back lots and examined them closely before going back to the street for his horse. The black was tired and needed a rest. He led the animal to the stable where Pete Lambert was standing in the doorway to the barn.

'Take care of my horse, Pete,' Bannon said. 'I need another mount urgently.'

'Sure thing! There's a bay that'll do you. What was all the shooting about?'

'I was tying up some loose ends.' Bannon led the black inside, transferred his gear to a bay, and rode to the rear of the jail. He began to follow the tracks left by Jex and Hendry.

It soon became obvious to Bannon that Jex was riding towards Owl Creek. He was concerned about Bella Thompson. He pushed the bay into a faster gait, his practised gaze easily picking out the fresh tracks. He really needed to be on the trail of Parfitt and the gang, but he also wanted some special deputies on hand to help capture the outlaws. Bella could send a message to the governor's office.

Evening was advancing by the time Bannon reached Owl Creek. He reined in on a slope with just his head showing above the skyline and studied the little spread beside the creek. Shadows were filling all the low places on the range and the sun was dipping for the western line. There was no movement anywhere around the ranch, and no sign of horses. He looked at the tracks he had been following. They went over the ridge and angled to the left, as if the riders were intent on bypassing the creek.

Keeping out of sight of the cabin, Bannon eased around the creek until he could see three horses hobbled in a stand of cottonwoods. A lamp was alight in the rear of the building. He reined in and dismounted, pausing only to check his deadly pistol before closing in on foot. Silence pressed in around him, broken only by the faint sound of water running over stones in the creek. He spotted movement at a rear corner of the cabin and froze when an indistinct figure stepped into view.

A wide-brimmed sombrero covered the man's face. He was holding a rifle in his hands and gazed around alertly as he circled the building at a slow pace. Bannon waited until the guard had passed around the opposite corner, then he sneaked in close to the back wall of the cabin. He tried the back door and found it locked. He went after the guard, moving cautiously, and discovered him standing at the front corner watching the trail. Darkness was closing in fast and shadows abounded.

The guard moved on around the corner to the front of the house. Bannon went after him, making no sound. He peered around the front corner, and froze when he saw the guard only feet away, standing with his back to the front wall. Bannon stepped around the corner, gun ready, and the guard whirled towards him. Bannon struck with his pistol, slammed the barrel along the Mexican's jawbone, caught the body and lowered it to the ground when the man collapsed.

Bannon lifted the Mexican bodily and carried him back around the corner of the cabin before walking away from the building until he was out of earshot. He lowered his prisoner into a depression, removed his weapons, and bound his hands behind his back with a neckerchief.

Full darkness was creeping in, and Bannon froze as he turned towards the house again, for a harsh voice was calling for the guard. He recognized Dave Hendry's voice and pushed his Stetson off his head for it to hang suspended down his back by the chinstrap. He picked up the Mexican's sombrero and put it on, its wide brim shielding his face, and walked in slowly, his gun-hand down at his side but ready for action. Hendry called again, impatience lacing his words. Bannon reached the front corner of the house and paused to look around it. Hendry was standing in the doorway of the house and lamp-light was shafting across the threshold.

'Are you asleep out here?' Hendry demanded, spotting Bannon's movement.

Bannon went forward. Hendry's big

figure was throwing a long shadow in front of the open doorway.

'Get the horses round front,' Hendry said, 'and be quick about it. We're going to Pronghorn Valley.'

Bannon reached the doorway. He peered at Hendry from under the brim of the sombrero. Hendry's right shoulder was bandaged, his arm hanging slackly at his side. He was carrying a gun but it was in a holster on his left side. Bannon made as if to pass the doorway and head for the creek and Hendry turned abruptly to re-enter the house. Bannon whirled, levelled his pistol, and stuck the muzzle against Hendry's back.

'Make a sound and I'll bust your spine,' Bannon said tersely. 'Get your hands up pronto.'

Hendry froze, then lifted his hands. Bannon snaked the man's pistol out of its holster. He prodded Hendry with his muzzle and the man went forward a few tentative steps. Bannon followed closely, crossed the threshold, and peered over Hendry's shoulder. He saw Bella sitting on a chair at the table. Mack Jex was standing over her with a knife in his right hand. Bannon saw blood on Bella's face. He struck Hendry hard with the barrel of his pistol. The hardcase fell to the floor and Bannon levelled his gun at Jex.

'You're giving me a whole load of trouble, Jex,' Bannon said angrily. 'So what are you doing here, and ill-treating Bella?'

As he spoke Bannon crossed the room to confront Jex, who dropped the knife he was holding and kicked it into a corner. He lifted his hands defensively as Bannon reached him, and was taken by surprise when Bannon lunged forward and shouldered him like a charging bull. Jex went flying and crashed into a corner. A board cracked under the impact and Jex slid down the wall to lie in a huddle on the floor. Bannon moved in and struck Jex with the barrel of his pistol, rendering him unconscious. He turned to Bella, and was relieved to see that she was not badly hurt.

'Jex is mighty unfriendly towards you these days,' Bannon commented. He examined Bella's face. She had a superficial cut across her forehead and a bruise around her left eye.

'He wanted to know if you were around here, and wouldn't believe me when I said I hadn't seen you,' Bella said unsteadily.

'Where's Cal?' Bannon suddenly missed the boy.

'I heard Jex and Hendry coming and sent him into the storm cellar.'

'I need a message sent to the governor's office. I want at least ten deputies out at Pronghorn Valley as fast as they can ride. There's a chance of catching Parfitt and the gang there when they return. When is the next coach due through here?'

'In the morning about ten. It'll come from Sadilla. The shotgun guard will take your message on to Hainsford and send it on from there by telegraph.'

'That's pretty slick. I'll tie my prisoners and take them back to Clarkville. You get my message off in the morning and then ride into Clarkville. It could be a mite dangerous around here alone until I've smoked the outlaws out.'

Bella did not reply. Bannon saw her cock her head to listen intently, and he caught the dull rumble of countless hoofs beating the hard ground. The noise grew like thunder in the hills, and Bannon checked his pistol.

'Cattle,' he said, frowning. 'Who's pushing a herd along at this time of the day?'

'Rustlers pass by here regularly,' Bella said. 'They're probably on their way to the hideout in Pronghorn Valley. It's Jex's business and you've got him here so why don't you ask him about it?'

Bannon moved to the door but Bella grasped his arm, shaking her head.

'Don't go out there,' she said. 'There'll be a dozen Mexicans with the steers, and you can't fight them all.'

Bannon nodded and they stood listening until a shot sounded just outside the rear door.

'That's a .22,' Bannon observed.

'Cal has got a squirrel-gun!' Horror sounded in Bella's raw tone.

Bannon started for the back door, as he reached it several heavy shots rang out startlingly clear and echoes fled across the darkened range.

8

'Douse the lamp,' Bannon rapped. Bella moved quickly to obey. As darkness swept into the building Bannon opened the back door a fraction to peer out. 'Stay inside,' he ordered, and slid out into the night to place his back against the wall.

He sensed rather than saw the moving cattle. Two riders had paused and were staring at the house. They moved on again, and Bannon watched and waited until the herd had passed. The sound of hoofs faded abruptly as the cattle dropped behind a ridge, and by that time Bannon's eyes had become accustomed to the soft darkness that now covered the range.

He saw a figure on the ground by the storm cellar and went to it, holstering his gun. Cal Garner was lying on his back with two dark splotches on his pale shirt-front. A .22 squirrel-gun lay by his side. There was a faint smell of gunsmoke in the shadows. Bannon dropped to one knee beside the boy and found him to be dead.

'Where is Cal?' Bella emerged from the house and came to Bannon's side. She uttered a cry and dropped to her knees, leaning over the boy's body and weeping softly.

'That first shot was from a .22,' Bannon said harshly. 'Cal must have heard the rustlers and come up out of the storm cellar to shoot at them.'

'It was a Mexican rustler who shot his father,' Bella said.

'How do you know that?'

'The Mexicans have been hanging around here for weeks. They made it plain what would happen if they were not allowed to pass without trouble, and Jex is in cahoots with them. He's behind this,'

'I'll take Jex back to jail,' Bannon promised, 'and catch up with the rustlers come morning.'

He went back into the house. Jex was beginning to move spasmodically in the corner. Hendry was still unconscious by the front door. Bannon saw a rope suspended from a hook over the fireplace and used it to bind both men. When they had recovered sufficiently to move under their own power he ushered them out of the house and dumped them with the guard. He fetched their horses from across the creek and mounted his bay, his movements deliberate.

Bella came through from the rear of the house just before Bannon was ready to ride back to Clarkville.

'I'll wait for the stagecoach in the morning,' she said, 'then I'll come into town. I can't stay out here any longer.'

'I was gonna suggest that.' Bannon nodded. 'It ain't fit for you to be here alone.'

He did not like leaving her but needed to get after the rustlers. He rode out with his prisoners and travelled at a fast clip to town, reaching the little community around midnight. There were few lights burning along the main street as he dismounted outside the law office, where the door was opened as he dragged Jex out of his saddle. Sheriff Bixby appeared in the doorway and regarded him silently as he ushered his three prisoners inside.

'Where did you pick them up?' Bixby demanded.

Bannon explained and Bixby snatched up his bunch of cell keys.

'I've got to hit the trail pronto,' Bannon said as they locked the prisoners behind bars. 'When I get back I wanta see these men still in here or you'll be in trouble. Have you got that, Sheriff?'

'They'll be here,' Bixby said grimly, nodding emphatically. 'I don't make the same mistake twice.'

Bannon gave more details of what had happened out at Owl Creek, then departed quickly. He rode out of town and angled across country, making for the distant Pronghorn Valley. Dawn found him riding steadily, and when the sun arose he looked around and changed direction slightly. When he ascended a ridge some ten miles from the outlaws' valley he reined in and looked around, his eyes narrowing when he spotted a herd of some 300 steers being hazed along in the direction of Parfitt's lair.

He shadowed the herd for awhile, noting the opposition. Six riders were pushing the cattle along and they were in no hurry. Bannon drew his rifle and checked its loads. He dropped back on a ridge and, when he moved forward again to observe the rustlers, he found one of the drag riders coming towards him. The Mexican started shooting as soon as Bannon's head appeared above the skyline.

There was no mercy in Bannon's heart as he drew a bead on the rider. He fired and the man slid out of his saddle. The crash of the shot hammered across empty space in a series of fading echoes. The cattle took off at a run in the direction of Pronghorn Valley, leaving a cloud of dust hanging in the bright air.

Bannon fired rapidly as the remaining Mexicans chased after the herd. Three of them went down quickly, and he spurred after the survivors as they disappeared into the dust raised by the fleeing herd. The cattle ran for a long time. Bannon rode to one side of their tracks to avoid the worst of the dust and, pausing eventually on a ridge, saw the cattle strung out on the rough ground with the two surviving Mexicans trying to gather them. He went forward quickly, determined to finish off the rustlers.

One of the Mexicans dropped back to challenge him. Bannon ducked when a shot crackled by his left ear. His Winchester hammered and the rustler pitched out of his saddle. He rode on, intent on getting the survivor, and was faintly surprised when the Mexican reined in, threw down his weapons, and lifted his hands in token of surrender.

Bannon closed in carefully. He reined

in beside the rustler, slid his Winchester into its boot and drew his pistol. The rustler chose that moment to reach to the back of his neck for the handle of a knife, and sunlight glinted on the blade as it was drawn. Bannon was not taking any chances. His pistol hammered and the slug thudded into the Mexican's chest. Blood spurted as the rustler fell from his saddle, and Bannon sat for a moment gazing at the rustler, his gun smoking.

The man was dead. Bannon listened to the fading echoes of the shot. He felt that he had avenged the death of Cal Garner, and grim satisfaction filled him as he went on towards Pronghorn Valley, deciding to check the hideout before returning to Clarkville.

When he neared the entrance to the valley he noticed the tracks of three horses heading in the same direction. The tracks were fresh, no more than a few hours old, and he wondered who was riding in to rendezvous with the outlaws.

He rode carefully through the narrow entrance and remained in cover where he could see the wide stretch of grazing-land that was hemmed in by bare rock walls. The valley seemed to be deserted but the three sets of tracks pointed in the direction of the shack shaded by the cottonwoods in the middle distance. He produced his field glasses and searched the area intently, quickly spotting three horses hobbled close by the shack.

It took Bannon almost an hour to work his way unseen to the creek beside the shack. When he had reined in under cover of the trees without betraying his presence he drew his Winchester and left the bay with trailing reins. The silence was intense in the valley and cattle were grazing peacefully on the lush grass. Bannon moved slowly, keeping the trees between him and the shack. He saw the three horses behind the shack, and paused when one of them lifted its head to look at him. It whickered softly before resuming its grazing. Bannon waited in the heavy silence, his Winchester ready in his hands.

He made it to the back wall of the shack without seeing anyone, and was filled with curiosity as he looked for a means of checking the interior. A convenient knot-hole drew him; he closed his left eye and peered through the hole with his right eye.

The interior of the shack was dim and he waited for his eye to become accustomed to the near-darkness. He saw two men sitting at a rough wooden table. They were conversing casually, and Bannon looked around for the third rider. He received a shock when he saw a woman roped to a chair in a corner and recognized Sarah Maddock.

What was she doing here? The question loomed large in Bannon's mind. Jex had tried to abduct her earlier, but Jex was safely behind bars now. Were these two more of Jex's men?

Bannon moved around the shack to the front door. There was no sign of Al

Piercey, who had been left earlier mortally wounded. He stepped into the doorway with his rifle in the crook of his left arm and his pistol ready in his right hand. Both men started violently at his appearance, but froze when they saw his weapons.

'Get rid of your guns,' Bannon told them. 'Do it one at a time and do it slow.'

The men obeyed. Bannon made them lie down on the earth floor with their hands outstretched. He went over to where Sarah was tied, his attention on his prisoners, and untied her.

'We'll talk in a moment,' he said. 'Let me take care of these two first.'

He bound both men and then turned to the silent girl, who seemed dazed by her predicament. She rubbed her wrists slowly as she gazed at Bannon with wonder in her wide eyes.

'What happened to you?' Bannon demanded.

'These two men came to my room in the hotel and forced me to go with them. I gathered from their talk on the way here that they work for Al Piercey, and picked me up on his orders to bring me here so Parfitt could get a ransom for me from my grandfather. But Parfitt isn't here, and Piercey was lying outside, dead.'

'Piercey?' Bannon was surprised. 'So that was his game. I wondered how he knew where to find this hideout.' He explained his first visit, which had resulted in Piercey being shot. 'He was stealing Parfitt's dough. So what made him suddenly decide to pull out?'

'We had a bad run-in over handling Sabre,' Sarah said. 'I didn't like the way he tried to take over. He wanted me off the ranch, and, when I went to Clarkville to be with Grandfather Piercey told me to stay there. But I stood up to him and fired most of the crew because they seemed to be behind Piercey. It looks now like I did the right thing.'

'We'd better get out of here in case the gang shows up,' Bannon said. 'Do you feel up to the long ride back to town?'

'I can't wait to get started,' she replied.

Bannon handed her his rifle. 'Just watch these two until I get the horses ready for travel,' he said.

He was concerned that Parfitt and the gang would return before they were clear of the hideout, and heaved a sigh of relief as they eventually cleared the valley and headed back to Clarkville. His two prisoners were roped in their saddles. They had nothing to say about Sarah's abduction when he questioned them, and maintained a grim silence during the long ride. Bannon made camp during the darkest hours of the night but did not sleep, and they were on the trail again as the sun came over the eastern horizon.

It was late afternoon when they spotted the collection of buildings that was Clarkville, and Bannon was exhausted when they reined up in front of the law office. Sarah slid out of her saddle and sat down on the edge of the sidewalk. Her face was grey and lined, and she could barely remain awake.

'Just rest there for a few moments,' Bannon told her. 'I'll see you to the hotel soon as I've jugged these two.'

'I need to visit the doctor's house to check on Grandfather,' she replied, getting to her feet.

'Wait for me,' he ordered, and she sat down again with a sigh.

The law office was deserted although the door was not locked, and Bannon ushered his prisoners inside. He called for Bixby but there was no reply. The cell keys were lying on a corner of the desk. He picked them up and ushered the two kidnappers into the cell block. When he found all the cells empty his eyes filled with a bleak expression, for Jex and Hendry should have been behind bars.

He locked the two men in separate cells and returned to the office. Sarah was standing on the threshold, leaning against a doorpost. She looked about all in, and Bannon went to her side.

'Bixby ain't here and the jail is empty,' he said, shaking his head.

'I always thought Bixby was unreliable.' Sarah shook her head as she gazed at Bannon. 'He never tackled the big issues facing the county. There was talk at times that he had to be in cahoots with the outlaws, the way he failed to do his duty. Perhaps he has pulled out, thinking his game is over.'

'Let's check on your grandfather and then you better get some rest.' Bannon escorted her outside and closed and locked the door.

He glanced around the street, which was practically deserted. There was a wagon outside the general store being loaded with supplies, and several saddle-horses were standing at a rail in front of the saloon. Two women were talking in front of a dress-shop. Bannon saw that one of them was Bella Thompson.

'You head for the doc's place,' he told Sarah. 'I'll catch up with you there.'

She moved away immediately, and he watched her as she crossed the street.

He saw Bella taking her leave of the woman in front of the dress-shop and went towards her. Bella saw him and came to him almost at a run.

'I'm so glad you've shown up,' she said when she reached him.

'What's the problem?' he countered.

'I came into town yesterday, and arrived in time to see Sheriff Bixby splitting the breeze, and looking like he wasn't coming back. Mack Jex and Dave Hendry were with him, and Jex wasn't acting like a prisoner.'

Bannon nodded. 'I guessed as much,' he mused. 'I've looked in the law office. The place is deserted, but there are a couple of deputies somewhere around, huh?'

'Not any more. They pulled out with Bixby. It looks like things were getting too hot for Bixby. I kept out of sight until Jex was well clear. I sent a message to the governor's office in Austin, and should have a reply by tomorrow, but I'll have to ride out to Owl Creek to get it.'

'You shouldn't leave town again until I've cleaned up the county.' Bannon heard approaching hoofs along the street and looked over his shoulder to see six riders reining in outside the saloon. 'Do you recognize any of those men?' he asked, dropping his right hand to the butt of his gun.

Bella gazed along the street before shaking her head.

'Where are you staying?' Bannon asked her.

'At the hotel. I'll be there if you want me.'

Bannon saw two of the riders turn and come along the street. They dismounted in front of the doctor's house. Bannon took his leave of Bella and strode along after them. They knocked at the doctor's door, and were awaiting a reply when Bannon reached them. He glanced at their horses and saw the Sabre brand on the animals. Both men looked at him as he paused beside them.

'Come to check up on Colonel

Maddock?' Bannon enquired.

'What's it to you?' one of the men countered.

'I took a job with Maddock a few days ago,' Bannon explained. 'I didn't see either of you at the ranch while I was there.'

'Are you Kelly?' the other man demanded.

'That's right, and I'm still doing my job. Sarah is here checking on her grandfather. I rescued her from a couple of Al Piercey's men. They kidnapped her and took her out to Pronghorn Valley.'

'Where is Piercey?'

'He's dead.' Bannon's tone was casual. 'What was Piercey up to? He was ramrod for the colonel, and yet he was working hand in glove with the outlaws. He had Sarah abducted and taken out to Pronghorn Valley to be held for ransom by the Parfitt gang.'

'That ain't all he's been doing. We've just ridden in from the north range, and two thousand head of Sabre cattle are missing from up that way. We ran into a bunch of rustlers, caught them red-handed, and shot the hell out of them. One of them told us, before he died, that Piercey was leading a double life — running Sabre while stealing it blind.'

The door of the house was opened and Sarah appeared with an older woman.

'Jack!' the girl exclaimed. 'Is Mason back with the rest of the men?'

'Sure thing. We just rode in. We got word about the colonel getting shot, and you wouldn't believe the half of what's been happening on the range. How's the colonel?'

'He's not out of the wood yet, but he's making progress. I want to talk seriously to Mason. Tell him to come to the hotel. I'll be waiting for him there.'

The two men turned away and went back to the saloon. Bannon watched them intently.

'Can you trust them?' he asked 'I saw six of them ride in a moment ago.'

'Charlie Mason is all right. I can trust him. He never saw eye to eye with Piercey. I'll talk to him — probably put him in the foreman's job at the ranch. He's often told me he could run Sabre better than Piercey.'

'And keep a couple of men close to you until I've dealt with Parfitt and his bunch,' Bannon suggested. 'I'll see you to the hotel and then you'll be on your own.'

'Thank you for what you have done,' she replied. 'If you need any guns to back up your play I'm sure Charlie Mason will help out.'

'I'll let you know if I need any help.' Bannon walked with her across the street to the hotel. He saw men piling out of the saloon and swinging into their saddles. They came at a canter along the street and reined up in front of the hotel where Sarah was standing. One of them dismounted and trailed his reins. He was tall and dark, his range clothes dusty and work-worn.

'Charlie,' Sarah greeted. 'I'm so glad

you're back. I need a good man to hold Sabre together until the colonel is back on his feet. Will you take over as the foreman? Piercey has gone.'

'I can sure do a better job than Piercey,' Mason responded, grinning. 'I'll take it on, Miss Sarah.'

Bannon turned away, satisfied that the girl would be able to handle her problems. He left them talking and went along the street to the saloon, thinking it was high time he set his mind on solving his own difficulties. He needed to set a trap for Parfitt and his bunch, and at the moment he had no idea where the gang was hiding.

He had a beer in the saloon before going along to the diner for a meal. After eating, and feeling the need for sleep, he went back to the law office with the intention of turning in there. He entered the office, locked the door, and was struck a heavy blow on the head. His knees gave way. He pitched to the floor as complete darkness fell upon him, and then he knew no more.

9

Bannon's first awareness of returning consciousness was a searing pain in his head which throbbed with each beat of his pulse. His eyes flickered open. He was in complete darkness. He lifted a hand to his face, wondering what had happened. All he could remember was that when he turned to lock the door of the law office it seemed that the roof had fallen in on him. He blinked but the darkness did not recede. He was lying on his back, and straw rustled when he rolled on to his right side. He was lying on a mattress.

He reached for his gun but his belt had been removed. He forced himself into a sitting position and pain swirled through his head. For long moments he sat with his head in his hands, waiting for the pain to recede, and became aware that the darkness was lighter to

189

his right. He saw the outline of a barred window and became aware of a patch of sky containing stars.

So he was in the jail! He pushed himself to his feet and staggered forward until his outstretched hand touched bars. He tested them with both hands, and a metal door gave slightly under his weight. He was in a locked cell. He wondered who was responsible for his predicament.

Bannon called loudly, and the echoes of his voice mocked him. There was no reply and he leaned against the bars and closed his eyes. He turned and staggered back to the bunk and lay down again. He slept until grey daylight filtered through the window.

When full daylight came he looked around the cell block. His head still ached but the pain had lessened considerably. His probing finger found a lump like a hen's egg on his skull and a patch of hair matted with dried blood. Presently he heard the sound of a key in a lock. He looked up to see the door between the cells and the front office opening. He gazed in some surprise at the slight figure of Sheriff Bixby. The lawman came to the door of the cell and paused just out of arm's length.

'What gives, Sheriff?' Bannon demanded. 'What the hell am I doing in here?'

'I panicked yesterday and made a run for it.' Bixby spoke heavily, shaking his head. 'Then I got to thinking that there was only one man standing in my way, and that was you. So me and the boys came back and waited in the office for you, and you fell into the trap like I figured.'

'So what happens now?' Bannon massaged his skull with gentle fingers. 'Turn me loose and I'll overlook your stupidity.'

'You're slated for a ride in the back of a wagon and a grave under a cut-bank out of town.' Bixby began to turn away. 'You know too much about what's going on. I had to turn Jex and Hendry loose yesterday, without a good reason for doing so. But this way, I don't need a reason. You'll just disappear and I can carry on as if nothing happened.'

'So the rumours about you being crooked are true, huh?'

'Yep. I know which side my bread is buttered on. I killed Jake Garner out at Owl Creek because he found out things about me, and last year I had to kill Bella Thompson's husband when I learned he was an undercover law man. Now you've showed up, and I got to put you out of the way, so don't waste your time tryin' to talk me out of it.'

Bixby turned and left the cells, leaving Bannon to gaze at the closed door while considering his predicament. A crooked sheriff would be hard to beat. Bannon crossed to the bunk, stood upon it to take a look out the glassless window, and saw the back lot, which was deserted. He remained on the bunk, watching for a passer-by. Almost an hour passed before he spotted Pete Lambert leading a horse.

'Hey, Pete,' he called, his voice

echoing. 'Come on over here. I wanta talk to you.'

Lambert looked around but kept going in the direction of the stable. Bannon called again. He stuck a hand through the bars, waved as he called yet again, and sighed with relief when Lambert turned suddenly and came to the window.

'What are you doing in there?' Lambert demanded.

'That doesn't matter,' Bannon said urgently. 'What is important is that I get out mighty quick. Have you got a gun?'

'Yeah, but I can't hand it to a prisoner.'

'Pete, if you wanta help the law like your father did then you'll give me your gun and then get a horse ready out back here for me to use. I have to get away. Help me get outa here and you'll be getting back at the men who killed your pa.'

'I'd like to, but I ain't sure I'd be doing the right thing.'

'Do you know Bella Thompson?'

'Sure.'

'She should be staying at the hotel. Go look her up, tell her I'm in here, and hear what she has to say about me. Make it quick, Pete. I'm due to be hauled outa here this morning. Bixby plans to kill me and bury me out of town.'

'I'll go talk to Bella,' Lambert promised.

'Make it quick, and tell Bella to bring me a gun to this window. Get a move on, Pete.'

Lambert nodded and departed. Bannon stepped down from the bunk and wiped sweat from his forehead. He paced the cell, counting the passing minutes, until his patience ran out and he stood on the bunk again, peering anxiously through the window.

The silence of the early morning was heavy over the town. Bannon wondered what was keeping Bella. She would surely come to his rescue. All he needed was a gun pushed through the bars and he'd get the drop on Bixby and fight his way out of this particular situation. He sighed in relief when Pete Lambert suddenly reappeared.

'I couldn't find Bella.' Lambert said. 'She left town early this morning — went back to Owl Creek. You want I should ride out there to talk to her?'

'Hell, no! That'd take too long. Give me your gun, Pete.'

'I can't rightly do that, you being an outlaw an' all.'

'Then go back to the hotel and find Sarah Maddock. Tell her I'm in here and ask her to get me out. She's got some of the Sabre outfit in town. Make tracks pronto, Pete. You know Bixby is crooked, and he's gonna kill me today.'

Lambert turned and departed. Bannon shook his head and sat down on the bunk, filled with frustration. He needed to be on the trail of the Parfitt gang. Time seemed to stand still while he waited, and he blamed himself for this situation because he should have done something about the crooked sheriff the minute he arrived in Clarkville and suspected Bixby of complicity.

Lambert called to him. He stood on the bunk and peered out through the window, to find the youth standing with Sarah Maddock. He explained the situation and saw doubt flicker into Sarah's face before he finished talking. She shook her head, and for a moment Bannon thought she was going to turn down his demand for a gun. But she produced a pistol and handed it to him between the bars.

'I'll see that your horse is waiting out here for you,' she said, and turned away with Lambert.

Bannon checked the pistol and found it fully loaded. The familiar weight of the weapon filled him with a fierce eagerness to do battle. He stuck the weapon in the waistband of his pants and pulled his shirt up to cover it before calling loudly for the sheriff. Bixby did not hurry himself, and tense moments passed before the door between office and cells opened and the sheriff appeared.

'Don't you feed prisoners in this jail?' Bannon demanded.

'It'd be a waste of time and money to feed you,' Bixby replied, advancing to the door of the cell. 'You'll be dead come noon. It won't hurt you none to go hungry.'

Bannon noted that Bixby was holding the cell keys in his left hand. He waited until the sheriff turned to leave and then drew the pistol and levelled it at Bixby.

'Sheriff,' he called urgently.

Bixby glanced over his shoulder. His eyes widened at the sight of the deadly weapon in Bannon's hand and he froze. His expression changed as shock struck him.

'Where'd you get that gun from?' he demanded.

'Come closer,' Bannon ordered. 'Let me outa here and you just might live to see the sun go down.'

Bixby hesitated, but the threat of Bannon's gun was too much for him. He came to the door of the cell and unlocked it. Bannon pulled the door open wide and snatched Bixby's gun from its holster. He dragged the sheriff into the cell and stepped outside to close and lock the door.

'Where are your two crooked deputies?' Bannon demanded.

'Around town, I guess.' Bixby sat down on the bunk. 'You won't get away with this.'

'What happened to Jex and Hendry?' Bannon persisted.

'They left town, and if they got any sense at all they'll still be running.'

'So what's been going on around here? You were in cahoots with Jex, weren't you? You're mixed up in the rustling that Jex has been running.'

'Not any more.' Bixby shook his head.

'So what about the Parfitt gang? How are you tied up with them?'

'I don't know what you're talking about. I never set eyes on any outlaws.'

'You've never tried to arrest any of the gang, and you were prepared to kill me to clear your trail, so you must be deeply involved. Come clean with me, Bixby, and you might be able to save something from this mess.'

Bixby shrugged and shook his head. 'Go to hell,' he rasped.

Bannon went into the office and looked around. His gun belt and pistol were hanging on a hook. Quickly he donned the rig and checked the pistol, reloading all chambers with fresh shells. As he turned to the street door it was opened and one of the deputies, Renton, appeared in the doorway. He paused and gazed at Bannon in disbelief.

'What are you doing out of the cells?' he demanded.

'Bixby turned me loose. He's taken my place in there, and there's a cell for you, so get rid of your gun and put your hands up.'

Renton saw that Bannon's gun was in its holster and his right hand slid to the butt of his own holstered gun. Bannon sighed, drew fast, and his pistol was cocked and pointing at Renton before the deputy could begin his draw. Renton halted his movement and raised his hands.

Bannon disarmed the man and ushered him into the cells. Bixby said nothing when Renton was locked in an adjoining cell.

'Where's your other deputy?' Bannon demanded. 'His name is Marsden, huh?'

'Go look for him,' Bixby retorted. 'I ain't his keeper. I'm through with law dealing.'

Bannon went back to the office and opened the street door. Sarah Maddock came pushing forward, with Pete Lambert and two tough cowboys around her.

'Thanks for coming to my aid.' Bannon returned the pistol Sarah had given him. 'I've got Bixby and Renton behind bars, and I want to get hold of Marsden.'

'I know where he lives,' Lambert said eagerly. 'I'll show you if you like.'

'Do you need anyone to stand by in the office while you're busy?' Sarah asked. 'Charlie will fill in as a deputy until you can get the law department reorganized.'

'Thanks. I could sure do with some help right now. When I've arrested Marsden I'll be able to get some honest lawmen in here.'

'Take over, Charlie, and stay while you are needed.' Sarah turned away, and the two cowboys entered the office.

Lambert led Bannon along the street, down an alley to the back lot, and paused at the door of a stout cabin. Bannon knocked at the door. It opened quickly in response to his hard knuckles. Marsden looked out at him, his deputy star gleaming in the morning sun.

'You're wanted at the jail,' Bannon said crisply, drawing his pistol as he spoke.

Marsden dropped his hand to his gun in a reflex action but stayed the movement when he found himself gazing into the barrel of Bannon's ready weapon. Bannon took Marsden's gun.

'Let's go,' he ordered, and Marsden walked along the street, his hands shoulder high.

'Thanks again, Pete,' Bannon said. 'Your father was a sheriff, you said. You can have a job as a deputy, if you like.'

'Sure thing! I'll go get my father's gun-rig and see you at the law office.' Lambert went off at a run towards the livery barn.

Marsden was put in the cells. Charlie Mason had made himself at home in the law office. He sat at the desk, his pistol lying on the desk-top.

'It's about time there was some real law around here,' Mason remarked.

'So what can you tell me about the lawlessness around here?' Bannon countered. 'Jex was running the rustling, they say, and Al Piercey was in with him. A lot of Sabre cattle have disappeared from the range. Did you see any of the rustling?'

Mason shook his head. 'I guess now I can see how it was done. Piercey ran two crews. I handled one of them, doing the usual chores around the range, and Piercey bossed the other crew. If stock was going missing then they were the men responsible.'

'You'd better give me the names of the men who were in Piercey's crew. If they're still around I shall want to talk to them.'

'I reckon you're too late as far as that goes.' Mason shook his head. 'Piercey's crew rode out when the colonel was shot. Piercey knew the game was lost by then.'

'I caught him in Pronghorn Valley, stealing Parfitt's cache of stolen money. I reckon Piercey was in cahoots with the gang as well as the rustling.' Bannon moved to the street door. 'I'm gonna take a look around the town. I need to see about getting extra lawmen in here.'

The door opened and Pete Lambert appeared, wearing a gunbelt and holster. He was excited at the prospect of being a deputy sheriff.

'What do you want me to do?' he demanded.

'Don't get too close to any of the prisoners while you're wearing that gun,' Bannon pointed out.

'Sure. I know what's what in this job. I watched my father a lot when he was the sheriff.' Lambert grinned. 'No one will get away with anything while I'm around.'

'Who is the mayor in this burg?'

'Frank Tolliver. He runs the freight line. You want me to show you his place?' Lambert moved to the door.

Bannon nodded. 'Yeah. You better stick with me this morning.'

As they left the office Bannon saw Sarah Maddock coming along the sidewalk. The girl was hurrying and she lifted a hand when she saw Bannon.

'The colonel wants to talk to you,' she said. 'I've told him what is going on in town and he said to get you.'

'Sure. We'll see him now. Pete, you

look up Tolliver and bring him along to the doctor's place to see me. Tell him it is urgent.'

Lambert went off and Bannon walked with Sarah to the doctor's house. The girl seemed strained. Her face was set and there was a frown between her eyes. They entered the house and Sarah led the way to an upper bedroom where Colonel Maddock lay propped up in a bed. The bullet wound he had received had taken great toll of him. He looked pale and ill at ease, and had lost weight. His face was taut, the grey skin stretched tightly over bone, and his eyes were filled with a trace of fever.

'Leave us, Sarah,' Maddock said as soon as he saw Bannon.

The girl began to protest but thought better of it and departed, shaking her head.

'I hear that you're an undercover lawman,' Maddock said harshly. 'It's about time something was done about the trouble around here.'

'I'm here to put the outlaws out of business.' Bannon spoke firmly. 'Perhaps you'll tell me about the strange set-up you've been running out at Sabre.'

Maddock shook his head. 'It's been like a nightmare. Is it true Al Piercey is dead?'

'He's dead.' Bannon nodded. 'I shot him.' He related the incident that had taken place in Pronghorn Valley. 'I suspect you were working with the outlaws.'

'Not of my own free will.' Maddock seemed to shrink in the bed. 'They had me over a barrel, and I went along with them because my granddaughter's life was at stake. She was used as a lever against me. Parfitt hid out on Sabre range most of the time, and I can tell you this — he's going to hit this town on the twenty-ninth of this month — the day the army sends its payload through to the bank here.'

Bannon stiffened. 'Is that on the level? Heck, that's in three days.'

'That's how it stood before I was shot,' Maddock replied. 'Parfitt is planning on taking the army payroll before heading for other parts. He reckons he's about played out around here. Can you get a posse together and set a trap for the outlaws? You'll need to lay your plans carefully. There's a man here in town who is watching for the gang. If he sees any signs of a posse he'll warn Parfitt and you'll never see him. This is the only chance you'll get to catch the gang flat-footed.'

'Who is the spy?'

'You can't pick him up. The minute you do that you'll lose Parfitt. You're gonna have to watch Joe Grant, and stop him sending any messages to the gang.'

'Joe Grant, huh?' Bannon nodded. 'What does he do around here?'

'He runs the local sawmill. Don't tip your hand to him or Parfitt and his bunch will disappear. You've got one chance to nail the gang, and I won't feel easy until the last one of them is dead or behind bars.'

Maddock slumped on his pillow and closed his eyes. Beads of sweat showed on his forehead as he gasped for breath.

'Keep an eye on Sarah,' he pleaded.

Bannon went to the door and called the girl. She came hurrying into the room and went to Maddock's side.

'You'd better stay under cover for a few days,' Bannon told her. 'Stick close to here and don't take any chances. I'll drop by and see you again.'

He departed, and met Pete Lambert and a large, fleshy man just outside on the street.

'This is Frank Tolliver,' Lambert introduced.

'I'm glad to make your acquaintance, Marshal,' Tolliver greeted. 'Pete was telling me what you've done so far. It's good to hear that Bixby's hold on the county has been broken. So how can I help you?'

'Charlie Mason is the new foreman of Sabre,' Bannon said. 'He's running the law office until you can get some new lawmen in there. Will you attend to that chore as soon as you can?'

'You bet I will! I know just the man to take over as the sheriff.'

'And put Pete in as a deputy,' Bannon said. 'I've got a lot to do right now, and I need to know the law can stand on its own feet while I'm away.'

'You can count on it,' Tolliver said. 'Come on, Pete. Let's get organized.'

Bannon watched them go off together. His thoughts were centred on Parfitt and his crooked bunch. He had much to do and little enough time in which to do it. He needed help, but fast, and wanted to contact Bella Thompson as soon as possible to set the wheels in motion. He turned towards the stable, intent on riding out to Owl Creek, and saw two riders coming along the street towards him. Both were holding drawn guns.

10

Bannon dropped his hand to the butt of his gun as the two riders opened fire. Slugs crackled and echoes chased away across the town. He dropped to one knee, drew his gun, and his eyes narrowed as he threw himself flat in the dust of the street and slipped into action. The two horses came straight for him, riders hunched in their saddles, weapons spurting smoke and hot lead. Bannon returned fire.

His first shot struck the rider on the left. The man twisted in his saddle and then pitched to the ground. Bannon shifted his aim to the second man. A bullet hit the ground in front of him, close enough to kick dust into his face. He squeezed his trigger and a slug struck the horse in the head instead of the rider. The animal went down in a slithering heap as if it had been pole-axed. The man tried to jump clear, but hit the ground hard and yelled in agony as the horse rolled on him. Echoes chased away across the town.

Bannon pushed himself to one knee, his keen gaze searching for more trouble as he reloaded his smoking gun. He stood up and walked to where the nearest rider lay trapped against the hard ground by the dead horse. The man was unconscious, his gun lying discarded close to his hand. Bannon kicked the weapon away and walked the few yards to the second man, who was lying on his face with a pool of blood forming in the dust beside him.

Boots pounded the street and Bannon looked around to see Pete Lambert coming towards him, gun drawn.

'I heard the shooting,' Lambert declared. 'What happened?'

'Take a look at these two and tell me who they are,' Bannon said.

Lambert thrust his Colt back into its holster and bent over the nearest man, grasping a limp arm to turn the body over. He straightened, his eyes glinting.

'Say, that's Ed Sawtell. He runs Mack Jex's ranch — M Bar J. That other guy looks like Bill Dodson, who works with him.'

'Jex again!' Bannon heaved a long sigh. 'I heard he took off for other parts. It looks like he didn't go far. Get a couple of horses saddled, Pete, and we'll take a ride out to Jex's ranch. With any luck we'll find him there.'

Lambert hurried away to the livery barn. Bannon watched townsfolk appearing from the buildings, drawn by the sound of gunfire. He holstered his gun, his thoughts busy on his assignment. There were some loose ends bothering him and the sooner he drew them together the better.

Charlie Mason came from the law office. The new Sabre foreman was wearing a sheriff's star on his shirt-front. He gazed dispassionately at the two downed men.

'Jex's riders,' he observed.

'Yeah.' Bannon nodded. 'I want Jex,

along with Parfitt's gang. I'll ride out to Jex's spread and look for him there.'

'Sure thing.' Mason nodded. 'I got control here. You go ahead and do what you have to do. Sawtell is coming to. I'll stick him behind bars and hold him until you get back.'

Sarah appeared in the doorway of the hotel. Bannon walked to her, on his way to the stable.

'Stay under cover,' he advised. 'I'm hoping to get to the outlaws today.'

'Do you think they might come here and harm the colonel?'

'There's no telling what they might do. You have to assume they will do the worst they can, so make sure you've got some trustworthy men around you.'

She nodded and Bannon went on. He entered the livery barn to find Pete Lambert saddling up two horses. Bannon checked his mount and led the animal outside. Lambert joined him, leading a black horse that looked as though it could run all day without getting tired.

'OK,' Bannon said when they were both mounted. 'Let's head for Jex's spread, Pete. We'll flush him out and settle him.'

Lambert grinned and headed out of town at a canter. Bannon looked around as they departed. He could feel an eagerness rising inside him, and pushed on resolutely. Lambert looked as if he was enjoying himself, and Bannon had to caution the youth to spare his horse. They cantered across good grassland and entered a range of low hills some miles out from Clarkville.

'Jex's place is about five miles from here,' Lambert observed.

'Pull into cover just before we reach it,' Bannon suggested. 'We'll look it over before riding in.'

Lambert nodded and continued. Eventually he reined in just below a ridge and dismounted. Bannon joined him and they bellied down before crawling a few yards to the crest to peer down a reverse slope. A small ranch lay huddled in a fold between two hills with a stream flowing quite fast into a creek. Bannon produced his field glasses and subjected the spread to a close scrutiny.

'It looks deserted,' he observed. 'There are no saddle-horses on the place. I think you should stay up here out of sight while I ride in to look around.'

Lambert objected but Bannon insisted, and the youth gave way. Bannon remounted and rode into Jex's ranch.

He reached the yard without incident and reined in at the porch.

'Anyone to home?' he called, and his voice echoed in the silence.

There was no reply and no movement anywhere. Bannon stepped down from his saddle and crossed the porch. He knocked at the door of the building and, when there was no reply, opened it and entered the house to search every room. He found them deserted. He left the house, and crossed to the bunk-house, which was empty. On his way to the barn to check it he paused to study hoof-prints in the dust of the yard, and dropped to one knee to peer more closely at the indentations he found.

Two sets of fairly fresh tracks led away from the corral and headed east. Bannon looked around, trying to guess at their destination. He straightened and waved to Lambert, and a moment later the youth appeared, coming at a gallop into the yard.

'Where do you think those tracks are heading, Pete?' Bannon asked, pointing to the ground.

'Owl Creek, I'd say.' Lambert looked around, nodding. 'Yeah. That's it. Are we gonna follow them?'

'I guess so. Who else could have made them but Jex and Hendry? We better split the breeze fast. Bella Thompson went back to Owl Creek this morning, you said?'

'That's right. She rode out at sun-up.'

'Then let's get moving. Bella won't want to be bothered again by Jex. Take the shortest trail to Owl Creek, Pete.'

Lambert set out and cut across the open range. Bannon noted that the tracks they had seen in the yard were heading in the same direction, and he began to feel concern for Bella. They had covered about five miles when he noticed a dozen sets of tracks coming from the south at an angle to those they were following, and his eyes narrowed when he saw where the bunch of fresh tracks swung to the east to follow those he supposed had been left by Jex and Hendry.

'Rustlers?' Lambert queried. He looked at Bannon with barely suppressed excitement showing on his youthful face.

'Could be, but I got a feeling Parfitt and his bunch left those tracks, and they're all heading for Owl Creek. This could be my lucky day, Pete. Say, look over there — two more sets of tracks following the main bunch! Who is trailing the gang? Hey, at last it looks like I'm in the right place at the right time. Come on. Let's go see who's out riding today.'

'If it is the gang you won't attack

them, will you?' Pete demanded.

'Give me half a chance to nail them and I'll take it,' Bannon replied.

They rode on, and Bannon was careful despite his haste. He had a vision of the gang riding into Owl Creek and catching Bella unawares. She had gone there to collect a message she was expecting from the governor's office, and he was concerned about her safety, especially if Jex and Hendry had gone there also.

'There's someone watching us from that ridge on the right,' Lambert said suddenly.

Bannon turned his head slightly and saw a rider reining back out of sight.

'Keep going as if we haven't spotted him,' he said quickly. 'I'll cut off in that direction as soon as I'm covered from his view.'

'What do you want me to do?' Lambert asked.

'Follow me at a distance and stay out of any shooting that may come our way.'

Bannon crossed a ridge and turned

218

to his right, staying just below the skyline.

He loosened his pistol in its holster and rode fast, ready for action, his keen gaze studying the ground ahead. He dropped into a dip in the ground and galloped up a long slope. A rider appeared above him, Bannon drew his gun and cocked it, watching for hostile movement. The rider lifted both hands to show that he was not holding a weapon. Bannon was surprised when he recognized Tom Arbuck, the bounty hunter.

Arbuck sat his mount and watched Bannon's approach, his heavily bearded face composed. When Bannon reined in beside him, Arbuck grinned mirthlessly.

'I've been watching you for some time,' he said.

'I saw your tracks way back,' Bannon countered. 'You've been trailing Parfitt's gang, huh?'

'Yeah. I went back to Pronghorn Valley after I took you into Clarkville and the sheriff gave me the lowdown on what you are doing under cover. I followed Parfitt's tracks out of the top end of the canyon and trailed him down to Sadilla. His bunch hung around there for a spell, and I picked up some whispers on what he's up to. Art Wiley is one of Parfitt's gang, and he can't hold his likker too well. I got him talking in a saloon and he told me there's a big army payload going into the bank in Clarkville any day now, and Parfitt is planning to grab it.'

'I know about that.' Bannon nodded. 'The money is due in Clarkville on the twenty-ninth.'

'I got a proposition for you.' Arbuck eased his weight in the saddle. 'I'll throw in with you and we can settle Parfitt's hash with no trouble at all — if we get him dead to rights. You said you can't claim the reward on any of the gang, so all you got to do is promise the dough will come to me and I'm your man. You can't handle the gang on your own, but between us we can knock them all off.'

'It sounds like you got it doped out right,' said Bannon without hesitation. 'I was gonna suggest something like that to you if I ran into you before reaching the gang. OK. You got a deal. It looks like Parfitt is riding to Owl Creek to lie low there until the twenty-ninth. There's a woman at the creek, and I want to make sure she's safe.'

'That'll be Jex's woman.' Arbuck nodded. 'I know about her. Do you know Jex is with Parfitt? I spotted him some time ago, riding with the outlaws like they are old friends. It looks like Jex is on his way to Owl Creek with the gang. What for has he thrown in with Parfitt?'

'Jex has been in business with Parfitt for some time.' Bannon shook his reins impatiently. 'Let's get moving and hit that bunch before they can get up to more helling.'

'Hey, hold up a moment.' Arbuck reached out a big hand and grasped Bannon's reins. 'I ain't going off half-cocked. I wanta know exactly what Parfitt's gang is worth before I tangle with them.'

'Between them, they're worth around ten thousand dollars. I added up their bounties when I started this assignment.'

'That's a handful of dough.' Arbuck nodded, grinning wolfishly. 'What about Jex? Is he worth anything?'

'Not to my knowledge,' Bannon replied.

'Then he's your meat. You can take care of him. OK, pardner. Let's ride.'

They went on. Bannon rode beside Arbuck and Lambert fell in behind, his expression showing uneasiness. A rider came out of a draw and Bannon recognized Arbuck's sidekick, who cantered towards them, grinning.

'You got a deal?' he demanded of Arbuck, and the bounty hunter nodded. 'Good. It looks like the gang is gonna hole up at Owl Creek. You want I should ride ahead and check them out?'

'I wanta do that myself,' Bannon said sharply. 'I represent the law and this will be done according to the rules.'

'You ain't gonna give Parfitt the chance to throw up his hands, are you?' Arbuck demanded. 'You know he ain't gonna do that nohow. Our only chance is to have an edge and then shoot the hell of out them.'

'If Parfitt plans to hit the bank in Clarkville on the twenty-ninth then he'll lay low out at Owl Creek until it's time to ride into town,' Bannon mused. 'That means they'll spend a night out here on the creek, and we should be able to take them around sun-up tomorrow.'

'I guess you're right.' Arbuck nodded. 'You want me and Bill to get round behind the creek to block a getaway?'

'You can stay back out of range until I've checked the area,' Bannon retorted.

Arbuck shrugged. They went on at a canter and miles slipped by under their fleeting hoofs. The trail of hoof-prints they had been following continued in the same direction. Early evening found them behind a ridge overlooking Owl

Creek. Bannon took his field glasses from a saddle-bag, left his horse in cover, and went ahead alone, using the contours of the ground to get in close without revealing his presence.

His first thought on sweeping the area with his glasses was that Owl Creek was deserted. There were no signs of horses anywhere. He checked the dozen or so tracks heading for the creek, and saw where they had entered the cover of the cottonwoods to the left of the cabin, still without seeing movement. When he looked around the yard and at the building he gained the impression that the place was deserted. Relief filled him when he considered that Bella might be back in Clarkville.

Even as the thought crossed his mind he saw the cabin door open and Bella appeared, followed by Rube Otter, one of Parfitt's men, who was holding a rifle. She was carrying a bucket and went to the well. Bannon watched closely. Bella looked as if she had come to no harm so far. She filled the bucket and returned to the cabin. Rube Otter looked around the yard before walking slowly on a circuit of the spread, eyeing his surroundings as he moved.

Bannon eased back down the slope to Arbuck and explained the situation.

'Mebbe the rest of the gang are holed up beyond the creek,' Arbuck suggested. 'They wouldn't wanta be too far away from their horses in case they have to make a run for it. Why don't you let Bill circle the creek? He'll soon nose them out. He's better than any Indian.'

Bannon glanced at the sky. The sun was well over to the west, and he estimated another hour of daylight before dusk.

'You stay put,' he said firmly. 'It's my job to look.'

Arbuck shrugged. Bannon went to his horse and swung into the saddle. He began a circle of the creek, staying off the skyline, until he reached the far side of the spread. He dismounted, left his horse in cover and scouted around carefully; picking up the tracks of a dozen horses where they had passed through the fringe of cottonwoods and continued over the nearest ridge. But he noted that four of the riders had dismounted under the trees and walked to the cabin. Their boot-tracks were plain in the patches of dust in the yard.

Bannon was aware that the outlaws would not be far from their horses, and he eased around the ridge until he could see the reverse of the slope up which the animals had traversed. He smiled when he saw a picket line with all the horses tethered to it. A camp had been made near the horses, and six outlaws were relaxing in it. Bannon was able to identify three of them as members of the Parfitt gang.

Full darkness came as he worked his way back to where Arbuck was waiting. He explained the situation.

'I'll take Bill and ambush those six in the camp while you and your deputy go into the cabin,' Arbuck said. 'Surprise them and they'll be easy meat.'

'I've got a better idea,' Bannon

countered. 'We'll sneak in on those in the camp just before sun-up and capture them, then close in on the cabin and take Parfitt.'

Arbuck considered the plan before nodding.

'That sounds about right. We need to take them on while they are split. OK. We are in business. You better settle down now and get some rest, Marshal, until it's time for action. Sun-up will be in about four hours. Too much moving around the creek will stampede the gang into running, and then we'd have a helluva job to catch them cold.'

Bannon nodded and hobbled his horse in cover. He sat down with Pete Lambert, tipped his hat over his eyes and relaxed, satisfied that he had done everything possible to ensure their success in the coming fight.

Grey light was beginning to crawl into the low places when Bannon stirred and looked up at the sky. He got to his feet, drew his pistol, and checked the loads in the cylinder. Pete Lambert was sitting nearby, hogtied and gagged. His eyes were wide and filled with despair. Bannon bent over the youth and pulled the gag from his mouth.

'What happened, Pete?' he demanded.

'That damn Arbuck jumped me. He's gone to take the outlaws in the camp and didn't want you getting under his feet.'

'How long ago did he set out?'

'An hour, I reckon. I ain't heard or seen anything since they sneaked away. He said he'd wait to hear you shooting at the cabin before he tore into the camp.'

Bannon was grim-faced as he untied the youth.

'Come on. Let's go take a look at that camp. I'll gut-shoot Arbuck if he makes a mess of this.'

They swung into their saddles and circled the cow-spread, making a silent approach to the outlaw camp. Bannon left Lambert in cover with the horses and sneaked forward alone to check. He looked for sign of Arbuck and his sidekick but saw nothing of them. Silence pressed in around him. Shadows were fading. He caught the gleam of a small fire in the camp and dropped to the ground to observe the scene.

A twig snapped just behind Bannon and he whirled, his gun lifting. He saw Arbuck only feet away, grinning. Bannon eased back, his face grim. He had counted only five outlaws in the camp, so one of them must have gone to the cabin. He cursed Arbuck for his recklessness and moved back out of earshot of the camp before whispering harshly to the bounty hunter.

'I'm going to the cabin now. Are you ready here?'

'Sure thing! I'll start shooting when you open up at the cabin.'

Bannon shook his head. He turned away and returned to where he had left Pete Lambert. Daylight was nigh and the sky to the east was streaked with crimson fire.

'Pete, I'm going to the cabin first. Bella is in there and needs to be protected. There's no telling what Parfitt will do if shooting breaks out here. He might kill Bella out of hand or try to use her as a hostage. Either way we'd be at a disadvantage. Are you ready to back me up?'

'Sure. Tell me what you want done and I'll handle it.' Lambert's voice was harsh with resolution.

'Just tail me and watch my back.' Bannon turned away from the camp and headed for the cabin.

The creek was noisy, rippling and washing over pebbles. The small natural noise concealed any sounds Bannon made as he stepped through the dust of the yard. There was dim lamplight spilling through the front window of the cabin, and Bannon wondered if Rube Otter was still outside on guard. He reached the side of the cabin without incident, and Pete joined him noiselessly.

Bannon moved to the front corner and peered around it. There was no sign of a guard. He drew his pistol and went on to the door of the cabin. He thrust the door open, stepped inside the building, his gun levelled. Lambert followed him closely. Bannon's quick gaze took in the interior of the cabin, and he was shocked to find the place deserted except for Bella, who was seated on a chair beside the stove, her hands and feet tied and a neckerchief stuffed into her mouth. She began making noises when she saw him, and motioned towards the back door with her head.

Moving swiftly, Bannon shot home the wooden bolt on the inside of the front door before crossing the cabin to the rear door and barring it. Pete hurried to Bella's side, removed her gag, and she burst into a torrent of explanation as he began to untie her.

'Parfitt and some of his gang were in here,' she said quickly. 'Then just before dawn one of the outlaws came in from their camp and said he'd seen someone prowling around the creek. Parfitt figured the law had arrived, set a trap

231

around the cabin, and you've walked into it.'

At that moment a harsh voice called from somewhere outside.

'You in the cabin. We got you dead to rights. Put down your guns and come on out with your hands up.'

Bannon motioned for Bella to get down on the floor, and pointed to a corner.

'Over there, Pete,' he ordered. 'Watch the back door and shoot anyone trying to come in. And keep an eye on that window.'

Lambert nodded and hunched down in a corner, his pistol steady in his hand. Bannon dropped to one knee by the stove, covering the front door.

'Are you coming out or do we come in after you?' Parfitt demanded, his raucous voice echoing in the tense silence.

Bannon tensed. The voice was coming from outside the front door. He raised his pistol and sent a slug through the door about waist high, which bored easily through the woodwork. Gun-smoke plumed across the cabin and the heavy crash of the shot reverberated. There was an immediate response from outside. Several guns opened fire and bullets smashed through the cabin walls, crackling and snarling in blind flight. The rear door came under siege. Someone began battering it with a heavy object. Pete Lambert fired several shots blind into the door and the attack subsided.

Bannon could hear the sound of rapid shooting in the background. He guessed that Arbuck and his sidekick were in action around the camp. The front window of the cabin was shattered and two men thrust guns through the aperture and emptied them recklessly. Bannon ducked as a slug burned the top of his left shoulder. He flattened out on the hard earth floor and returned fire, his bullets smashing into targets which he could not miss. A bearded face fell away from the window with blood spouting from it. The second man swung his pistol to line up on Bannon, but Lambert fired from his corner and the man, yelling in agony, dropped from sight.

The back door of the cabin swung open and an outlaw appeared with two levelled guns in his hands. He triggered his weapons and cooking utensils on the stove jumped and clanged. Bannon swung his Colt and fired quickly, sending two shots into the man's chest.

Heavy gun echoes began to fade. Bannon pushed himself to his feet, faintly surprised that he was still alive.

'Watch the back door from your position, Pete,' he said. 'I'll go out the front door and circle round to the back to check. Don't shoot me by mistake, huh?'

'You got it,' Lambert replied, reloading his pistol.

Bella got up from the floor and picked up a rifle.

Bannon broke his gun and reloaded swiftly. He moved to the front door and opened it with a quick motion. A gun blasted and the bullet smacked into the door. Bannon lunged outside, throwing himself to the ground and swinging his gun around to cover all angles. He glimpsed Hank Parfitt only yards away, lying on the ground, spattered with blood, and trying desperately to lift his weapon.

'Drop it or you're dead,' Bannon called.

Parfitt showed his teeth in a snarl of defiance and continued to lift his gun, using both hands. His shirt-front was soaked with blood. Bannon fired, sending harsh echoes across the range. Parfitt jerked, flattened out, and lost all interest in fighting.

Bannon got to his feet and looked around. Two outlaws were lying dead by the front window. He went to the right-hand corner of the cabin and passed along the side to the rear corner. Three outlaws were down in the dust around the back door. Bannon nodded. It looked like Pete Lambert had avenged his father's murder.

He glanced towards the creek and saw Tom Arbuck standing on the knoll where Jake Garner and his son Cal were buried. The bounty hunter waved a hand and Bannon acknowledged. Arbuck turned to busy himself loading dead outlaws on horses.

Bannon looked around, suddenly noticing that the wooden door of the storm cellar was open. He levelled his gun, walked towards it, and was barely yards from it when the head and shoulders of a man appeared from inside. Sunlight glinted on a pistol the man was holding in his hand, and Bannon set his teeth into his bottom lip when he recognized Dave Hendry.

'Drop it, Hendry, and come on out,' he called.

Hendry ducked, and then came up shooting. Bannon squeezed off a shot and Hendry fell backwards out of sight into the cellar. A yell came from inside the cellar.

'Don't shoot. I want to give up,' a voice shouted.

'Sure thing, Jex,' Bannon replied. 'Come on out with your hands up and I'll take you prisoner.'

Jex appeared from the storm cellar, his hands shoulder high. Bannon went forward to check him, keenly aware of the heavy silence pressing in across the range. Pete Lambert appeared with Bella in close attendance. Both were unhurt. Bannon heaved a long sigh and his mind began to descend from the high plateau of alertness demanded by the showdown. It came to him then that his assignment had ended. Parfitt's gang was down in the dust and the gunsmoke had faded. Owl Creek was back to normal.

THE END

BOTH SIDES OF THE LAW

Hank J. Kirby

A full hand in draw poker changed Hardin's life — and almost ended it. First there was the shoot-out with the house gambler. Then suspicion of bank robbery, enforced recruitment into a posse, gunfights in the hills and pursuit by both sides of the law in strange country. He'd never had so much trouble! What should he do? Drift on, away from this hellhole, or stay and fight? There was no real choice — it was fight or die . . .

LIZARD WELLS

Caleb Rand

After losing his whole family to a bloodthirsty army patrol, Ben Brooke takes to the desolate Ozark snowline. Years later, he returns to the town called Lizard Wells, where the guilty soldiers have degenerated into guerrillas, bringing brutal disorder to the town. Also living there is the tough Erma Flagg — and more importantly, Moses, a young Cheyenne half-breed . . . After a wild thunderstorm crushes the town, Ben, in desperate need of help, chooses to step single-handedly into a final reckoning.

MISFIT LIL FIGHTS BACK

Chap O'Keefe

Misfit Lil wouldn't allow the rustlers to run off some of her pa's improved Flying G beeves. She started a stampede that trampled them bloodily into the dust. But then two assassins gunned down horse rancher Sundown Sander's son Jimmie. And he had made no move to defend himself, despite Lil's stormy ride to bring him warning. Could devious madam Kitty Malone or gambling-hall owner Flash Sam Whittaker tell the truth about Jimmie's fatal resignation? Lil had to find out.

SHOOT-OUT AT BIG KING

Lee Lejeune

Billy Bandro arrives in Freshwater
Creek in Wyoming to start a new life
away from riding with the killer
outlaw Wesley Toms. When Toms
is captured, Billy is assigned to
drive him to Laramie for trial, but
Toms' gang bushwhack the coach,
leave Billy for dead, and take
Nancy Partridge and her Aunt
Emily hostage. The gambler Slam
Beardsley saves Billy, and they
ride off in pursuit. But there are
many surprises for them in the
mountains . . .